THE OUTPOST FILES

By: John Seay, Sean Lewis

PROLOGUE:

9/11 had changed everything for America. People became scared, paranoid, and even reckless with their actions. Luckily patriotism gave people a sense of unity. Through unity people were given a place. Somewhere to be safe and there was safety in numbers.

It is why the military develops a strong sense of brotherhood. Our best come together and form a bond that can and will be tested by man, time, and the unknown. It is the dark times that bring them together, remembering their training. What they have been through and how they get through what they jokingly call "The Suck". They can fight anyone and anything at any time. It is why they are the proud and the elite. Time and time again their brotherhood and courage will constantly be tested. It is why soldiers call each other not comrades but brothers. Because they know they got each other's back and together there is no force that can tear them apart.

The kitchen window framed a dying day, streaks of crimson bleeding into indigo as night crept in. Stellan's eyes fixed on the horizon, but his mind was a thousand miles away. His fingers drummed an anxious rhythm on the countertop, shoulders bunched tight as coiled springs. The looming deployment hung over him like a storm cloud, dark and inescapable.

As he looked on into the waning day giving to the night, it was all a reminder he was going to have to go. It was the weighing feeling of how long it would be. If everything went right, he could be gone at most three to four months. Then if everything went the way bureaucrats and desk jockey's way, he may never be back.

The gentle touch on his back startled him from his spiraling thoughts. He turned, meeting Abigail's warm gaze. Her presence seemed to soften the harsh edges of reality, if only for a moment.

"Hey," she said softly, her hand lingering on his back. "You, okay?"

Stellan managed a tight smile that didn't reach his eyes. "Yeah, just... thinking." He was a soldier of fortune not a thesaurus.

Abigail's brow furrowed with concern. "Is it about the deployment?"

He nodded, running a hand through his short-cropped hair. "Can't seem to get it out of my head. Everything is happening all at once. This war has and is going to change me, I know it will. Then if I come home…"

"When you come home," Abigail sternly corrected.

"When I come home, I'll have this little guy looking to me. Like I'm his father or something."

"We'll know when the test comes back!"

Stellan laughed, "That's not funny."

"Yeah, it is." She loved to make Stellan laugh. He enjoyed it too. Reminded him he was human and not just a drone the military trains to fight and kill.

He continued to smile, even if he had to force it as he was now. He did it for her. He knew he needed to smile for her. She did everything for him, and damn it, the least he could do was smile for her. It was literally the only thing she wanted. Aside from the kid.

Unfortunately, she often knew when he was faking it. The weight of unspoken fears hung between them. The unknown and the uncertainty of the future was opaque. He wished he was a clairvoyant; being able to tell Abigail what was to come and happen. It would make things all so much easier. They could plan, they could prepare, they would be ready for anything. But the reality was. He could not control reality. No one could.

"I know it's what I signed up for," he finally said, his voice low and rough. "This is something I have to do. It's not just for myself. I want to do our country proud. I want this world to be a better place for our child." He turned to Abigail and smiled. This time it was real, and she was grateful.

Abigail's hand found his, squeezing gently. "Stellan, you're one of the strongest men I know. You will have your bothers with you."

"Damn right I will. Best men anyone could ask for and I'm lucky to have them."

Stellan's mind began to wonder again, and Abigail could see he was drifting off into another silent void. She decided to cut through the heavy silence, her tone deliberately light. "Hope you're ready for the trip." She said, laying a gentle hand on his arm. "Got everything packed yet?"

Stellan blinked, caught off guard by the sudden change of subject. "Uh, yeah! I think I do" he replied, his voice rough." He laughed, "When am I not prepared?"

"Yeah, right," Abigail doubted her husband's prep work. She knew him since high school. Hard worker, but also the hard worker who puts everything to the last minute too.

Stellan nodded, a mix of gratitude and reluctance etched across his face. "Yeah, I guess it'll be good to get out there with the boys." He said, trying to move his thinking forward. His fingers drummed an erratic rhythm on the countertop. "Being out in the open will do me some good."

"It's going to be fun!" Abigail wandered over to the fridge and began to eye her next prey. "Promise you'll at least try not to think about the end of world while we're out there."

"You're right," he admitted, as a real smile emerged this time. "It's just hard to switch off sometimes, you know? To stop thinking about what's coming." He looked to her; she was still waiting for an answer. Somehow it reminded him of his drill sergeant, except he liked looking at her more.

"I promise." He said, his voice low and resolute, "This is going to be a simple and fun trip."

CHAPTER 1

The desert stretched endlessly before Stellan, a vast expanse of sunbaked earth and jagged rock formations. God, he loved El Paso. He relaxed his grip on the steering wheel, eyes constantly scanning the horizon. The rumble of engines behind him was a comforting reminder as his friends, their wives, followed in a tight convoy. Dust billowed in their wake, obscuring the road they'd traveled.

He said nothing as Abigail was listening to the music. He couldn't recognize who sang the song. It was that hippy hop music. He preferred the sound of country any time. But every once a while he did catch a good rhythm with it, but he enjoyed this time. He didn't have to say anything to her. She was there and that was enough for him.

He stayed vigilant and watched the road with ease. As they continued down the dusty road in the distance, he could see something running out in the open. Switching from the road to the animal he saw it was a coyote running. He had seen many of them when on training or their runs during training. But this had to be the biggest he had ever seen. Maybe an alpha male, though those don't really exist. He could see why researchers would make such an assumption.

"Look at that thing." Stellan said to Abigail. See leaned forward to see what he was looking at. "Look at the size of that son of a bitch."

"I've heard they could get big."

Then the coyote was joined by a couple others the same size. Abigail dismissed it, but Stellan kept an eye on them. He had never seen coyotes that size before. He tried to keep an eye on them but had to look forward to making sure he didn't miss his turn. When he looked again, they were gone. It vanished it seemed like.

"Weird." He spoke. How could he lose sight of something that friggin big? He slowed his truck down and made the sharp turn with ease. As he turned, he made another look to catch the running pack again. They were gone. He didn't just lose sight of them. He couldn't even see anything out there. As he thought of it, he hadn't seen any other animal out there this whole time. No birds, or even desert critters like a lizard.

Years of military service had honed his instincts to a razor's edge, and right now, he was feeling that things were off. He thought maybe his thoughts of deployment were getting to him and allowed himself to dismiss it. But not entirely.

Stellan's gaze darted to the rearview mirror, checking on the vehicles behind him. His friends' faces were visible through dusty windshields, everything looked fine.

***

They arrived at what they called the Outpost. It was an older place, something that people had forgotten long ago. It was the sight of a former cavalry outpost, but it burned down some time in the late 1800s. Since then, there had been others who came out to rebuild it. For a while it was part of Fort Bliss as a weapons range but sold off to someone in the last fifty years or so. Stellan happened to be a friend and was given permission to go out there. Just if they agreed they wouldn't sue him if they got hurt doing something stupid out there.

His friend had plans for it a couple of times, but nothing ever happened. Now it just sat there, and Stellan was sure he and his friends were the only ones who ever visited the place. It held a certain charm, like a fix me up type of charm. But really this was probably its full potential.

Stellan surveyed the land as his friends pulled up. He was looking for those coyotes again, but he was just met with silence. It was quiet as always, but he just couldn't shake the feeling that this place had somehow changed since he was last here.

"Grab the chairs." Abigail called out to Stellan. Surely, he didn't expect his pregnant wife to be lifting things.

"Right! I'll be just a minute."

6

Abigail watched him as he made his way to the back of the truck. The others were pulling up now. She rolled her eyes as she watched Stellan scanning the area like a soldier. "Just please have fun." She spoke. But he couldn't hear her.

The vehicles ground to a halt in a cloud of dust, their engines falling silent. His friends and their significant others were helping them unpack. Stellan got a camper seat out for Abigail. He went back and fetched the cooler; Asher was there to help him out.

"You waiting on me?" Stellan asked.

Asher nodded. He was the oldest of the friends. He had more experience than the rest. He didn't like the idea of being a leader, he was more of the behind-the-scenes type of guy. He didn't say much, but Stellan made it a habit to listen. Asher always seemed to know what to say to make him feel better or teach him something new.

"You doing, alright, brother?" Asher opened.

"Yeah, why wouldn't I?"

"Like I wouldn't know." Asher always knew. For a quiet guy he married opposite to a woman with a big mouth. The only thing bigger than her mouth was her ears. And Abigail always told her everything. No doubt Asher would hear it and needed to do something. It's how most of their conversations started.

"Okay," Stellan surrendered. "I got a couple of things on my mind."

"I'm not going to lecture you or tell you things you already heard." Asher replied. "Doesn't do anyone any good to be told what they already know. Or what they don't want to be told."

"I'm always listening."

"I was with you on our first deployment. I know what you are like."

"And?"

"Enjoy what you got right now. You're not on a drill. You're not training. You're not even doing mock missions. You're here enjoying yourself and the time with your friends and family."

The others began to unload, their laughter and chatter feeling oddly out of place in the oppressive quiet. Stellan found it hard what Asher was telling him. He understood what he was saying, but the meaning was just not making a landing.

"This silence," he replied quietly, "it's not natural. Even the damn wind seems afraid to blow."

"Not sure what that means. But you need to relax. This trip is more about Abigail, so suck it up."

Stellan nodded. He looked over to Abigail who was relaxing. She was with Asher's wife, Lauren. He was sure she was telling her everything that he didn't want her to know. Luckily, Abigail knew what to say and not to say.

"Stellan!" Asher's voice cut through Stellan's brooding. "Get your head out of your ass and let's do some damn camping already."

"Sorry, just lost in thought."

Asher clapped him on the shoulder, his grip firm, with a small chuckle, and reassuring. "I know that look, little brother. You're wound tighter than a newborn Iraqi goat. Everything will work out. Trust me."

***

The campfire crackled, its orange flames casting long, dancing shadows across the desert floor. Stellan sat rigid, his back against a weathered rock, eyes overlooking the landscape. He felt much better tonight. He was able to distract himself with his friends and setting up camp kept his mind busy and focused on something. He thought about what Asher had said. This trip was for Abigail, and all day he kept her on top of his thoughts, and this too helped him relax.

His friend, Chip, was quipping about something. He always had some funny story. Were they real? Sometimes, and sometimes they weren't. They were all funny as hell and it made him, and his friends laugh. He imagined Chip being a comedian if he hadn't joined the army. Nothing huge, but enough to crack out a living maybe at the local bars. He was out there with his fiancé, Alice. She was a lot like him, and Stellan couldn't imagine what their life at home was like. Probably just played pranks on each other all day.

Then there was Liam with his wife, Marie. They had been married for two years now, just three behind his and Abigail's. Nothing so great about Liam, just your routine grunt who met his wife on an outing with the guys. Clyde and his girlfriend were there too, just a quiet guy you could share a drink with. Then there's Barks. He thinks he's a werewolf. That's it. Nothing to add there.

Looking out into the twilight, Stellan forgot about the oppressive silence of the night pressing in around them, broken only by the occasional pop of burning wood. Though it bothered him he could not hear any crickets or cicadas chirping out there. He felt it was strange he did see any birds either. It was as though wildlife was trying to stay away from here. He didn't want to think about it as he looked back to Abigail. It was a nice night, and he was not going to let a weird feeling get in the way of her happiness.

Like Asher said: Tonight, is about her.

The night continued until Clyde caught everyone's attention.

"Guys," Clyde's voice was low, urgent. "Something's here."

The laughter around the campfire died instantly. Stellan was on his feet in a fluid motion, muscles tense.

"What is it?" Lauren whispered.

"Coyotes," Stellan breathed, his eyes never leaving the encroaching ring of glowing orbs. "But... something's not right about them."

"Easy, they're just animals." Chip replied as he slowly got up. He didn't underestimate coyotes hunting in packs. They were canines, but they were also clever.

The eyes moved closer, revealing lean, shadowy forms. A low growl rumbled through the night air, raising goosebumps on Stellan's arms.

"They spooked or something?" Asher muttered, suddenly at Stellan's side.

Stellan's mind raced. This was impossible. Coyotes didn't stalk humans, especially with such calculated precision.

"What do we do?" Alice asked, panic edging into their voice.

Stellan swallowed hard; his mouth dry. "Don't worry. We got this." The initial disbelief quickly morphed into palpable alarm as the coyotes slunk closer, their guttural growls reverberating through the camp. "Get the guns." he spoke softly. He didn't want to rile up the animals any further.

The others did as Stellan said. They kept their rifles close by. It was instilled in their training to keep their firearms nearby, and they often enjoyed popping off a few rounds at the outpost. It was all part of being prepared for anything that can and will happen.

Stellan's mind raced. This wasn't right. Coyotes didn't behave like this. But there was no time to puzzle it out.

"Asher, on three." Stellan ordered, shouldering his rifle. "Hold and only fire when you get a clear shot. They're too close for a mistake to happen."

Chip's shots rang out, sharp cracks piercing the night. Stellan squeezed off controlled bursts, aiming for the glowing eyes. But something was off. The coyotes seemed to shift and waver, making it impossible to get a clean shot. How could they be this quick?

"They're not dropping!" Barks yelled. Calm, but the panic was there.

"Doesn't seem like they want to leave," Asher added.

Stellan's heart hammered against his ribs as he watched a coyote take a direct hit. At least he thought it was a direct hit. The shot came from Asher, and he was the best one in the group.

"What the hell?" Stellan muttered, blinking hard.

"Stellan, you see that?" Asher's voice was tight with disbelief.

"Yeah," Stellan replied, his mouth dry. "I saw it. But I don't believe it."

Stellan did not like how this was unfolding. Usually when you hit something, it fell. These things just kept jumping around them.

"Damnit!" Liam yelled out. "They're just fucking with us!"

"This isn't making any sense." Clyde said aloud.

"They should either be attacking or fleeing. Not this dancing bullshit or whatever they're doing!" Asher said.

Stellan couldn't believe what he was witnessing. These were just average animals, right? He sighted another one hoping he had just mistaken the miss shot for what it was. He eased up at the impossible sight of a coyote vanishing into thin air. It clashed violently with everything Stellan thought he knew about physics. Wasn't much, but he still knew nothing could just vanish and reappear without reason. As he stared into the darkness, finger tense on the trigger, Stellan felt the foundations of his world begin to crack under everything he feared.

Stellan's training warred with the surreal nature of the situation. His muscles tensed, ready for action, but his mind struggled to process what his eyes were seeing.

"We're running low on magazines even!" Clyde said.

"This isn't possible!" Stellan growled, squeezing off another round. The bullet passed through a coyote as if it were made of smoke. "What the hell are we dealing with here?"

Asher's voice, strained but steady, cut through the chaos. "Stellan, we're running low on ammo. These things... they're not natural."

Stellan's jaw clenched. "I know. But we can't just--" he looked to Abigail and she to him. She shook her head.

Then it happened. Stellan's rifle clicked. He looked to the others, and they had nothing. They too had run out. That's when the coyotes stopped their jumping and began their circle.

"What is this?" Stellan asked himself.

The coyotes stopped and turned their heads towards the sound of air being chopped in the sky. Stellan and his bothers looked where the coyotes looked. In the distance they saw a bright light heading their way.

"Chopper!" Asher yelled, his voice barely audible over the approaching thunderous rotors.

The largest of the coyotes turned to Stellan and their eyes met. Stellan looked closely and saw its eyes shift to a dark brown and then back to glowing gold. He opened his mouth to say something, but then the creature raised its head and howled loudly. Everyone covered their ears. Stellan thought he was going to bust an eardrum.

The chopper flew over as it the pilot saw nothing. Stellan and the others looked up as the powerful beam from the chopper's spotlight cut through the darkness, revealing... nothing. Where moments ago, there had been a sea of snarling coyotes, now there was only empty desert.

Stellan blinked, momentarily blinded. "What the fuck..." he started before the realization hit him. "Everyone okay?"

11

As his friends called out, shaken but unharmed, Stellan's mind reeled. The coyotes, the impossible vanishing act, and now a military helicopter appearing out of nowhere – none of it made sense. But one thing was clear: they were leaving.

***

They did not bother with proper protocol and abandoned their training to throw everything they had in the back of Stellan's truck. Stellan didn't even bother breaking down the tent. He was sure that Chip just left his out there. He was speeding down the road with his friends following.

"What the hell just happened?" Abigail finally broke the silence.

Stellan shook his head, his voice barely above a whisper. "I don't know, man. But whatever it was... it wasn't normal."

"No shit!"

"Get some rest," Stellan instructed, his tone brooking no argument. "I'll take first watch."

Stellan said nothing else as they headed back to the safety of their homes. He looked over to his stressed wife as she held her stomach. When they were back on the highway, he eased up on the speeding. He was relieved that Abigail and their unborn child were unharmed. As he concentrated on getting them home. He reflected on what happened. He wasn't sure what to make of it, but he was going to find out.

CHAPTER 2

Stellan awoke the early dawn; it was time for him to get back to the base. He kissed his wife and bid her goodbye for the day. His time off the base was up. She said something as she struggled to wake up but failed. He knew through her grumbling and mumbling it was something of a mixture of, "I love you too" and "Damnit, let me sleep."

On the base he worked as a military police officer with Asher and some of the other guys who were at the outpost last night. He stopped by his house where Asher was already waiting for him. He got in with a nod. As usual he was a man of very little words, and he always means well.

Together they drove in silence. Whether it was instinct to do so, or this was what their friendship looked like was anyone's guess. They did everything together and a lot of it was in silence, but when words needed to be exchanged, Asher had plenty of vocabulary words to share.

"That shit sure was strange." Stellan was the first to speak. He knew Asher wouldn't bring it up again unless someone else said it first.

"It sure was. Never seen coyotes that big and act so strangely."

"They had plenty of opportunities to kill us too. I don't know why they didn't go into the kill."

"More than anything, it was like they wanted us to use up our ammo."

"Like they just wanted to scare us off?"

"Seems that way."

They did not live far from the base, and it took no time to find their office. And of course, the sergeant was there waiting for them, and it was never a good thing when they saw him.

Stellan knew it meant what he called *bad news* and *badder news*. He just hoped it wasn't about anything he forgot to do. Last time he screwed up, he had to hold to paint cans up at his side, and each time he let them drop it was another mile Asher had to run. It was only funny once and never again when Asher couldn't feel his legs and Stellan, his arms. The *badder news* was they had to find out some shit and that always took forever that led to nothing at all. In other words: shit work.

"Good to see you." He started, but that was a lie. "Last night a hiker went missing."

Stellan and Asher said nothing. They were too well trained to say "so?" or "Isn't that job for the cops?"

"It was near our base. Which means we are asked to look into it." The sergeant went on. "Get out there and see what happened. A got damn mountain lion probably ate a hippy."

"Probably trying to make it eat a celery stick."

"That's what I think. One less vegan in the world means one less problem in the world, I say."

"We'll find him."

"Good. Write a report and we'll call it good. I know you two are shipping out in about a week. I figured this was just a day's work." The sergeant dismissed them. "Do your country proud but at the government's pay." He joked as he left the room.

***

Asher and Stellan took to the road in their military hmmwv. It was nice to be in a four-wheel drive since they had a lot of terrain to cover.

"This could be a good chance to check that place out." Asher was the first to talk about the weird shit this time.

A little surprised, Stellan replied, "Really?"

"The old outpost is in our jurisdiction and things got weird as fuck out there."

"It really got to you, didn't it?"

"Hell, yeah it did. We are the few but the proud. Army of one and all that cool shit. You think I'm going to let a fucking mutt put me in my place." Asher spat. "I went through hell to get where I am. Who the fuck those dogs think they are?"

"What we do? Guns can't kill 'em."

"Fuck that. I'll stomp a chocolate mud pie in its ass and serve it in the god damn mess hall."

Stellan laughed. There were only a few times he had seen Asher get this worked up before. He would be lying if he didn't feel the same way. Fuck those dogs.

As the day waned on, they did all the proper routes and saw nothing. It was getting late into the afternoon and the evening was going to set in. When they decided to head back to the outpost like they have said.

That was when Stellan spotted it.

"The hell is that?"

Asher turned and before he could ask "what?" out of human habit, he already saw what Stellan was looking at when the jeep came to an abrupt stop.

The looked down and saw something shinning catching their eyes. They had been down this path many times but never saw anything like this before. It gleamed from the sunlight, almost like it wanted to be seen. Stellan already didn't like what he was looking at when he pulled a pair of binoculars to his face. There was a strange-looking totem, at least that's the best work Stellan could think of. It looked as though it were attached to a person.

"Fuck."

"Yeah, that looks bad."

"I mean there's there no road down there."

"Awe shit!" Asher knew what this meant.

The two got out of the jeep and packed what they needed for the hike down to the corpse. It was not easy as the merciless sun beat down on their necks as they trudged on. Waves of heat shimmered off the cracked earth, distorting the horizon. His boots crunched against loose gravel, each step a reminder of the unforgiving terrain. Asher slipped, but Stellan caught him. He did not look forward to the trip up and the last thing he needed to do was to have a large man strapped to his ass while doing it.

They managed though, but it was neither fun nor easy. Stellan preferred flatness. He hated stairs and he hated broken escalators. Life would be so much better without mountains.

15

"Look alive. Mountain lions can be anywhere." Asher reminded Stellan.

"There it is though."

The two approached the corpse. They did not like what they were seeing. They had found their guy alright, and no animal could had done this. At least a natural animal of nature.

Stellan took a step back from the sight. Asher did the same. They went out there prepared to see a mauling. Stellan had Asher had seen pictures of people and animals killed by animals. This was an entirely different thing.

This guy had been hallowed out completely and then stuffed with strange plants. His body was contorted in different ways and shriveled. His blood was drained completely. but what haunted them was his eyes. They were completely intact and left behind. They too were shriveled, but this was due to dehydration. Not bloodletting.

He starred out at them with face of pain and torture, forever frozen in the last feeling he had before he died. His mouth, unhinged with his teeth and tongue taken.

Stellan and Asher were saddened and horrified that this was done to a human by another human.

Seeing a dead body was one thing when you are a soldier. It is still completely different when it's a murder. It was thought that entered Stellan's head. When you got to war, you plan to kill the enemy. They are doing the same thing. Even if you don't want to be there. It was the nature of war to bring soldiers there to kill enemy soldiers. Murder was so much different through.

This guy was out minding his own business, and someone did this to him. He was out hiking, enjoying his home where he thought he was safe. Then this happened to him. Someone wanted to hurt and end his life simply because they could. No sense of honor, respect, or decency. They did this to him and left him naked and posed this way.

"Jesus, help us all." Asher said after he gathered himself.

"We'll need to call this in."

"Let's look around first. Make sure we have the scene covered."

They surveyed the area, but the only thing that was out of place was they hiker's clothes were folded neatly and set to the side. Not a single drop could be found.

"Whoever did this, had plenty of time to do it."

"There's no sign of struggling either."

"This isn't making any fucking sense." Asher said in frustration.

Stellan was silent for a moment. "Just more of a reason to check out the outpost."

"I was thinking the same damn thing." Asher agreed.

Normally Stellan didn't investigate things. He had heard stories of UFOs, Sasquatch, Nessie, and jackalopes. He didn't believe in any of that shit. Crazy people looking for attention or some drug addict thought an alien came across the galaxy to look inside his asshole. To him it was all bullshit. Stuff like that didn't happen.

Then one night a couple of abnormal sized coyotes fuck with him and his friends. God only knows what happened here.

There was no way these two events coincided at the same time. Everything happens for a reason. There are no coincidences; especially when shit like this is involved.

***

Asher phoned it in as Stellan continued to look around and took pictures of the man. God, he hated that his happened to him. Sure, the hiker could have had someone mad at him. Sure, he could have gotten into the wrong crowd. But this. This messed up shit should never happen to anyone.

"Why didn't you fight back?" Stellan whispered to the dead man. "Could you fight? Didn't you want to?" He asked knowing he would not find his answer here. Dead men tell no tales.

Night was about to fall soon as the El Paso police department, homicide detectives, and even a Texas Ranger came out to the scene. Everyone looking for answers and asking questions.

He and Asher had lost count how many times they said the same thing over. Of course, they knew what would happen would be they all would comb over the verbal details looking to see if they were hiding something or just flat-out pulling shit out of their asses.

17

However, this was no longer their case. It was now in the hands of the law and a future prosecutor. But this was not going to stop them. They knew something strange shit was going down and if they had said so. Then they would either been kicked out of the military.

After all, how would it sound if they explained they felt that large coyotes killed a guy and made him into a scarecrow because they had nothing else to do. Stellan knew he would be kicked out of the military, and then on some stupid ass show on the Sci-Fi Channel trying not to look like an asshole with couch potatoes laughing at him. Or worse, agreeing with him because the same thing happened to them.

They did what they were told to do. They found the missing guy and wished they hadn't. Stellan took the wheel this time. It was his turn to drive.

It felt that it took longer to get to the outpost. Maybe it was because of the dead body they saw. Maybe they didn't like the idea of running into the coyotes again.

"I ain't getting out unless I know those coyotes are not around."

"Oh hell no. I'll drive them over and see if they can dodge that."

The two shared a laugh. It was more of a nervous laugh, but it was good to laugh after what they had been through. It made them feel a little bit better, but that good feeling was not going to last much longer.

As they approached the dirt road leading to the outpost there was a man standing there with an AK-47. He sported a gray cap and gray jacket over black tactical style Caro pants and black combat boots. What really stuck out was a upside down four-leaf black clover logo on both the hat and jacket.

He put his hands up in the air to bring them to a stop, which Stellan did.

"Howdy, stranger." The man greeted.

"Sup!" Stellan said as casually as he could. He didn't want to start trouble with a guy who was already armed and ready to fire. Stellan didn't like him being out here and this calm while holding a high-power rifle.

"You boys need to turn around and go about your business."

"Just checking out a couple of things, sir." Asher replied with a sense of authority in his voice.

"Not here, you ain't." The man said with more forceful tone. The tone Stellan did not like to hear in a man's voice who is armed with a high-power rifle.

The man took in a deep breath and let it out in a frustrated sigh. Stellan could see he was not used to anyone, not even military men in uniforms, disagree with him. "Well…" he stopped to think of what to say. Stellan could tell he was a man not to be vague. "What are you checking out?"

"There was dead body not found too far from here."

"And?"

"Well, there places to hide up there."

"Not tonight there ain't." The man insisted.

"I'm sorry, but we can't take your word on that."

The man narrowed his eyes on Asher, not liking what he had to say. Stellan was starting to feel a lot more aggression coming from this guy. He looked around. At this time a man dressed the same way got out of the truck.

"These boys giving you trouble?"

The guard waved his friend back and waited until he was back in the truck. He turned his attention to Stellan and Asher. "Wait right there. And I damn well mean it." Stellan nodded because he could tell he damn well meant it.

The window to the truck lowered, revealing there were three others in the double cabbed truck. Stellan knew they were watching him and Asher closely. Asher slowly withdrew his side arm, preparing for the worst.

"Shit just keeps getting shittier." Asher said.

"I don't like this." Stellan said. "If they look at me wrong, I'm punching it."

"Right."

They watched as the man spoke into a comm device. Looked like he was talking into this fist. He leaned further in the truck to hear the reply. It was only about five minutes but felt like forever for the guard to finish. He picked up his rifle and shouldered it as he walked back over to the jeep.

"Alright." He started. Stellan could read the look on the man's face. He could see things would have been easier for him if Stellan had turned around like he asked. "You're free to come take a look. But don't take long. If I have to go up there to make you leave, I ain't going to be nice about it." He finished as he backed up.

"Thank you, sir." Stellan said. He would have apologized but the man was looking away for any other visitors and waving him on already. He did not look like he was in the mood to get to know them and so he went forward.

***

Asher was right that shit was getting shittier.

Stellan and Asher were amazed at what they were seeing. As they got closer to the outpost things had changed from the night before. They pulled up to their old camping site and saw new structures were put up. Flood lights were illuminating the area and generators buzzing with power making sure everything was working. IT guys swarmed the comms tent. Soldiers were marching in formation. Others were jogging to get to their post. Makeshift towers were up in four areas with snipers on the lookout for trespassers.

A black jeep with a large upside down black clover with a white outline on the door, leading two other identical jeeps, honked at Stellan so he knew not to move as they passed him. Then a truck passed them carrying men with rifles as well. They were dressed differently from the guard at the entry post. These guys were wearing black and gray camouflage bearing the same clover on their breast and center of their helmets.

Stellan and Asher got out and started looking around, amazed at what they were seeing. What really got their attention was in the distance, something was really taking place. With the use of binoculars, Stellan saw them at work. Black chinook covered over a large area, lowering down supplies to a group of people. On both sides of the large chopper were two little birds armed and ready.

"The fuck is going on?" Asher asked.

Stellan said nothing as he surveyed the site. There were excavators, dump trucks, bulldozers, and cranes all working on something. He didn't know what they were doing. The only obvious thing he could make out was that they were digging for something.

He passed the binoculars over to Asher. "Take a look. They're digging and I don't know what it is."

"Like I would know." Asher said as he began to look.

Stellan watched as everyone in the area were scrambling to get somewhere. Trying to get things to work. Doing something that needed doing. It was all strange, but a cold shiver went down his backside. He quickly turned around, not wanting to see the guard again. But when he did, he saw nothing by the barren land. Everything looked boring compared to what was happening behind him. Yet, he could feel like he was being watched.

"I think we need to go."

Asher lowered the binoculars about to tell Stellan they still had some time, but he could feel it too. He could feel the eyes of those coyotes again. He could feel them watching him and Stellan and every move they were making. Hell, he figured they even could see what they were about to do before they even did anything.

"We need to beat it."

"Right."

They got back into the jeep and took off. The jeep skidded on its wheels as he frantically turned the jeep around and high tailed it out of there. They got to the post again and were stopped by the guard.

He signaled them to roll down their window. He smiled as he looked at Stellan and Asher, both looking pale and like they've seen a ghost. He nodded. "You boys find whatcha you're looking for?"

Stellan did not like that smile. Luckily everything from training came back to him and took over his nerves and thoughts. He never thought his training would ever be needed in a situation like this.

"Yes, sir." Stellan said in a clear and calm voice. This took the guard's smile off his face.

"Well then I reckon you boys need to leave." He said sternly.

"Thank you for your cooperation." Stellan said, meeting the guard's eyes.

The guard drummed his hands on Stellan's door and took a step back. Stellan did not like this guy being so professional before, and he sure has hell did not like his less professional behavior now.

"The only thing I can tell you is this." He stopped and returned to his more professional pose. "You just pissed the covenant off."

"The fuck does that mean?" Asher asked.

The guard said nothing else and just stared at them with narrowed eyes and smirk on his face. Stellan did not like that at all. Stellan did not want to hear his answer and decided to leave while they were still letting him. Stellan took glances at the mirror until the guard was out of sight. They stopped at a stop sign and waited for the oncoming traffic to stop.

Stellan waited until to go when he felt Asher backhand his chest.

"The hell?"

"Shut up and turn your head." Asher said with an easiness tracing his words.

Stellan turned his head. He saw something standing not too far from their jeep. It was the same sensation he felt back at the outpost looking at the dig site. It was this thing that was the source of that cold chill. It looked a man standing there, but it was no man. It was one of those coyotes and this time it was standing on its hind legs. It was strange. It had the knees of a normal human. But its body was covered in shaggy fur, and it had human hands. Its head though, was that of a coyote. As it watched it looked like it was changing more and more like a human.

"Oh! Fuck me…" Stellan said.

"Go!" Asher said.

Stellan shoved the pedal down with his foot. The wheels spun in its place until they were able to grab something hard. The jeep leapt out on to the highway and Stellan didn't bother looking back. Two nights in a row with him speeding away trying to get away from that damn outpost.

Shit just keeps getting shittier.

CHAPTER 3

The chow hall buzzed with hushed voices, the clatter of utensils against trays a stark contrast to the tension hanging thick in the air. Stellan's eyes darted between his companions, noting the creases of worry etched into their faces. He stabbed at his eggs; appetite lost to the memory of last night's eerie events.

"Those weren't normal coyotes," Barks muttered, his usually booming voice now barely above a whisper. "The way they moved, how they just... disappeared."

"Not this again!" Clyde complained as he finished his meal.

"I thought we weren't going to talk about that anymore." Chip interjected.

Stellan nodded, a chill running down his spine. "There's more that's happening up there. Asher and I checked it out."

"Yeah?" Clyde asked. Not really encouraging this conversation but was interested.

"Yeah, there's some group up there."

"Who?" Chip asked.

"I don't know. I've seen them before. Some kind of paramilitary group."

"Government contractors." Clyde snorted. He never liked them and thought it was just money spent on stupid shit he felt funneled money away from more important projects. But it was always the same. Some guy's nephew is given the money in Washington because of the Good Ol' Boy System. He gets in there, has a rich friend that wants to make more money and get power, gets a contract and then the next thing you know the military can't buy something simple like armor for your Humvee.

Asher leaned forward; his brow furrowed. "Come on, guys. There's got to be a logical explanation."

"You two come in here. Say something about big coyotes and saw one standing like a total rando and you want a logical explanation?" Chip replied.

"There's nothing logical about any of this." Clyde added. "Look at Stellan over there. He doesn't believe in anything. The fact that he's even a Christian at all is a miracle of God."

"What you want from us anyways?" Barks asked.

"Asher to help us figure out what's going on at the outpost area."

"Shit, I don't know, and I don't want to know." Chip answered. He really didn't want to. Especially learning that some paramilitary organization was now involved.

Stellan wished he could share his friend's skepticism, but the knot in his gut told him otherwise. What the hell are we dealing with here is all he could think of. Coyotes standing up and he was sure that any day one will be in the office working casually and just turn to him and be like: "Sup?" Hell, none of this was making any sense.

"I just want to know what's going on." Stellan finally said in frustration. "They are about to send us to Iraq to look for weapons of mass destruction and this is happening in our backyard. For all we know this is a terrorist cell that is home grown."

"I'm telling you its government contracts." Clyde insisted. "If it was something nefarious, I'm sure we would have been mobilized and done something about it."

"But its Americans that are doing it." The only thing Barks could think of to make is sound okay.

"And that's what pisses me off about it!" Stellan stood up slamming his hand on the table. The entire mess hall got really quiet. Stellan saw every soldier and officer was looking at him. He sat back quietly and began again, "I'm just saying that there's a credible threat to everyone here."

"I agree." Said Asher.

"We can't overlook this because they're Americans. Anyone is capable of being evil. Whether for money or power. As if there was anything else to temp men."

"What about a woman." Chip laughed.

24

"Bros before hoes." Clyde replied. They all shared a good laugh about that, which helped break up the tense conversation.

"Seriously, you guys. There's something happening here in El Paso. I don't know what and I don't want to leave my pregnant wife alone here with them. I don't want any of your wives or girlfriends alone here with them. Just think about everyone you care about. Your family, your loved ones, friends, and their kin folks. Can you really be okay being on the other side of the world with this weird shit happening so close to home."

"Remember…" Asher was careful with what he was about to say. "The whole damn reason we're going to Iraq is because they said we are fighting them over there, so we don't fight them here."

"And they may already be here." Stellan concluded.

"Well fuck, it's probably nothing." Barks replied not liking the smell of what Stellan and Asher were cooking up.

"I really hope it's fucking nothing. I really do." Stellan said. "But what if it isn't."

"Listen to yourself." Chip said. "You really think that this is about wizards and dungeons and dragons?"

"Maybe…" Stellan said not really wanting to admit that maybe there were things in this world that neither science nor religion could explain. Maybe this world was more than what it seemed. He was a Christian man. It was all supposed to be living by the Bible. Being a good person. Being a good neighbor. Living by the lord's desire and praising him. Then when you die you go to Heaven and the sinners bake in Hell. Now this is here, and he doesn't know what to think.

Exasperated by this conversation Chip cleared his throat, a mischievous glint in his eye. "You know, if you want answers, there's always the Sleepy Deer."

"What now?" Barks asked, raising an eyebrow.

"It's this old bar about an hour and half from base," Chip explained, his tone lightening. "Real hole-in-the-wall type place. But man, the stories you hear there..."

Stellan's curiosity peeked. "What kind of stories?"

Chip grinned, leaning back in his chair. "Oh, you know, the usual. UFOs, government conspiracies, things that go bump in the night. It's where all the local kooks go to swap tales."

Clyde snorted. "Sounds like a goldmine of reliable information."

But Stellan couldn't shake the feeling that Chip might be onto something. He glanced at Asher, seeing the skepticism on his friend's face. How do I convince him this is worth checking out?

"Look," Stellan said, his voice low and intense, "I know it sounds crazy. But after what we saw last night, can we really afford to dismiss anything?"

Asher held his gaze for a long moment, then sighed. "Fine. But I hope this turns out to be nothing but ghost stories and swamp gas but while we're there you can buy the drinks."

"He can buy your drinks." Chip said.

"You're not going?" Asher asked.

"Nope. We got about a week and half before deployment. I ain't spending it going on a witch hunt."

"You?" Stellan asked Clyde.

He shook his head. "You guys want to know more about this. I don't. I'm out."

Stellan and Asher looked to Barks. "Sorry guys! Full moon tonight and I'm meeting with my pack!"

Stellan looked over to Asher. "I guess it's you and me and I'm buying drinks."

"How the fuck did I get into this?"

"Because you're my best friend."

"I'm your only friend and you treat me like shit."

***

The sun dipped below the horizon as Stellan and Asher pulled up to the Sleepy Deer bar. A real hole in the wall like Chip said it was. Its outside weathered wooden exterior, faded dreamcatchers and peeling paint murals adorned the walls, hinting at a once-vibrant celebration of Native American culture now worn by time and neglect. At the top SLEEPY DEER burned in neon with the L blinking on and off. Signs that any time its life would end, and probably happily.

Stellan's eyes traced the intricate patterns, this place looked sad and creepy at the same time. Not at all how he imagined it when Chip was talking about it. "This place looks like it's seen better days," he muttered.

Asher killed the engine, his usual bravado noticeably subdued. "Yeah, well, let's hope it's got some answers to match its charm."

As they approached the entrance, the weathered door creaked open, revealing a dimly lit interior. The atmosphere shifted palpably as they stepped inside. A haze of smoke hung in the air, mingling with the rich scent of aged wood and something Stellan couldn't quite place – a hint of sage, perhaps? Low conversations hummed around them, punctuated by the occasional clink of glasses.

A couple of barflies stayed hunched over the sides as the bartender did the very minimum of his work. Others stayed at their table. Probably been there for days and nights. Asher felt sure that most of them probably just lived there now.

"Jesus," Asher whispered, his eyes adjusting to the gloom. "It's like stepping into another world."

"More like a bathroom."

Stellan nodded, scanning the room. The patrons were a mix of weathered locals and what looked like drifters, their faces half-hidden in shadow. "Make you wonder what Chip was doing up here."

"Stealing stories to pass off as his own. Or better yet, he got lost and ended up here for directions."

"I believe that."

They approached the bar. The bartender stared at them for a moment. Then he realized that Stellan and Asher were waiting to be greeted. He sighed. "What will it be?"

"Just two beers. I don't care which."

The bartender reached under and pulled out two Blue Moons. Asher was disappointed but he figured it was better than anything else he had under there. He was hoping for DosXX but really, he just wanted to leave.

Stellan leaned on the bar towards the bartender.

"Watch it, Bub." The bartender warned. He did not like his patrons getting too cozy with him.

"My bad." Stellan backed off. Trying to play it cool. "I was just wanting to know something, and I was told I could find out about it here."

"Looking for those weird ass stories? You from the SyFy Channel?"

"No."

"Good. Sick of a-holes coming in here and harassing everyone."

"I know right? We're from the army base over in El Paso."

"Didn't take you guys to be lawyers."

Stellan chuckled. "Alright, but I was told I could find out some stuff about animals acting weird."

"Standing up on their hind legs weird."

"You get that a lot."

"He isn't the vet. But there's a guy in here that knows shit about that." He pointed his head over to a table where a large man with long black hair sat. A big fucker at that too. After seeing him, Stellan was really hoping it would have just been a burnt-out college teacher. "We call him Bear."

"What's his real name?" Asher asked.

"Bear. That's why we call him Bear." The bartender answered as he put a fireball on the bar. Asher sighed as he grabbed it. "This is the drink you're buying him. He's a cool guy that's why we let him stay here."

"How cool?"

"He owns the bar. That's why we let him stay here."

"Of course." Asher said. "Thanks." He said the bartender nodding his head to the tip jar. Asher dropped a five in because he was enjoying the atmosphere so much.

***

Stellan's eyes locked onto a figure seated alone at a table in the center of the room. The man's presence was magnetic, commanding attention without uttering a word. His long black hair cascaded over broad shoulders, framing a face etched with lines of wisdom. But it was his eyes that truly captivated – dark, introspective pools that seemed to hold the weight of generations.

"Figures he would look like this." Asher muttered, nudging Stellan. "Bear, right?"

Stellan nodded. "That's what the guy said." His jaw tightening. Something about Bear set him apart from the other patrons, an air of quiet authority that both intrigued and unsettled him. "Let's approach carefully," he whispered. "We don't want any trouble."

Asher, ever the charmer, flashed a disarming smile. "Mind if we join you?" he asked, his voice carrying a warmth that belied their trepidation. Bear's gaze shifted slowly from his drink to the two men, his expression unreadable. Stellan tensed, ready for any reaction. But Bear pointed at the fireball in Stellan's head. "It's for you."

Bear gestured to the chair across the table from him as he took the fireball. He opened it and slugged it down in as if were nothing. He took out the whole bottle like it was made of water. He wiped his mouth and looked at Asher and Stellan with his dark eyes. Stellan felt nervous. He had never actually met a Native American before, and the first one he met was definitely a badass.

He leaned in, his voice low. "We're looking for some information about—"

"Why are you whispering? No one here cares about you or what you want."

"Sorry."

"This is not the movies. Just ask me what you want to know and leave me alone."

Stellan and Asher looked to one another.

"Look at me. He does not know what you want to know. If he did, he would not be sitting here, and you would not be trying to buy me off with whisky."

"I'm sorry."

"Do not say you are sorry. If a man does nothing but says he is sorry, then that is all he will ever be: is sorry."

"You're right. I…"

"I know why you are here," Bear interrupted, his tone measured and calm. The words hung in the air, heavy with unspoken knowledge. "Just remember you are an outsider to me. This is my domain. Not yours or your country's."

"Well, it's all America." Asher said.

"No. It was land taken from my people. You are offering me a fireball. The drink that has dispelled my kind for generations. I own this bar you and hand me a drink I own. You probably believe I call it firewater still. Then offer it to me as a gift? Who the hell you think you are?" He raised his voice as he stood up towering over Stellan and Asher.

They looked to one another. Everyone in the bar began to look at them as Bear's words began to rise. They didn't understand how this all went so badly. This guy could be their only lead to what's going on and they just insulted him.

"I'm…" Stellan couldn't find the words to apologize with. Especially since Bear just told him to not say he was sorry.

"The bartender said…" Asher was completely lost and dumbfounded. He thought at any moment Bear was going to start swinging and neither of them wanted to fight Bear. Then he thought about how others would react to two MPs getting into a fight at a bar with a Native. This shit looked bad, and the media was going to make it worse!

Bear sat back down. "It is a joke."

"What?" Stellan asked in disbelief. Especially since Bear did not change his facial expression.

"I am only fucking with you."

Everyone in the bar started to laugh. Asher and Stellan laughed nervously as they realized that this guy was cool. Stellan exchanged a glance with Asher, whose easy smile had faltered slightly. What have we gotten ourselves into? Stellan wondered, steeling himself for whatever revelations awaited them in this dimly lit corner of the Sleepy Deer.

**

Bear's dark eyes fixed on Stellan, piercing through his soul. There was something about Bear that was just inhuman. It was like he was sitting across from an emissary from God. He could not help being in awe from the aura that surrounded this man. Stellan felt that maybe there was more to this world, and Bear was more in tuned to it than he ever would be.

"This world is old. It holds secrets older than time. Not only domesticated secrets but secrets from other places as well." He intoned; his voice a low rumble that seemed to make the very air vibrate. "Secrets that don't like to be disturbed."

"I believe that."

"And you should with great caution." Bear said as the bartender sat down some water next to Bear.

Stellan leaned in, his heart pounding. There was something in Bear's words that resonated with the unease he'd felt back at the outpost. "What kind of secrets?" he asked, his voice barely above a whisper.

"Do not make this weird, soldier."

Stellan sat back up. "Sorry." Then Stellan closed his eyes at the word sorry.

"It is okay. And I will allow that. Sometimes it is okay to apologize. Don ot take everything you hear to heart. I just want to you be aware of how you sound."

Asher shifted uncomfortably beside him. "Come on, man. We're not here for ghost stories," he scoffed, but Stellan could hear the nervous edge in his friend's voice.

"I know. I had received a call from my friend, Chipply."

"You know Chip?" Asher asked. Curious to know. Not many people called Chip by his last name since he was born as Matthew Chipply.

"He has come in a couple of times with his bullshit stories. But they are fun to listen to. He called before you came to make sure I would be here."

"Makes sense." Stellan said. Also explains how Bear claimed to know what they were here for.

Bear's gaze shifted from Stellan to Asher. "The coyotes you saw... they are but messengers. Harbingers of what's to come." He paused, letting the words sink in. "The helicopter... it disturbs me more."

Stellan felt a chill run down his spine. He wondered how much Chip told him. He opened his mouth to ask, but Bear continued.

"There are forces at work here, beyond your military might. Ancient spirits that do not take kindly to... intrusion."

Asher let out an exasperated sigh. "Look, we appreciate the local color, but we're dealing with real-world problems here. Do you know anything or not?"

Stellan shot his friend a warning glance. He wanted to hear what Bear had to say. Asher was about to say something else. "Dude! Shut up!" Stellan muttered, "I want to hear this." He turned back to Bear, his mind racing. "What kind of intrusion are we talking about? And how does it connect to what we've seen?"

Bear's expression softened slightly, a flicker of approval in his eyes. "I thought it was just nonsense too. That was until you arrived. I could smell their scent on you, and it is strong."

"What is it?"

"I will tell you soon." He leaned forward, his voice dropping even lower. "Beware the men who seek to harness powers they do not understand. They think like the white men in the days of old. They believe they have the power to manipulate and control ancient forces."

Stellan's throat went dry. The weight of Bear's words seemed to press down on him, stirring memories of the eerie stillness that had preceded the coyote attack. He wanted to dismiss it all as superstition, but something deep within him recognized the ring of truth.

Bear's eyes locked onto Stellan's, his gaze penetrating. "I am the son of a healer. For generations my ancestors have helped keep a balance between the physical and spiritual realms. Each year it becomes more difficult with the rise of greed and enabling technology."

Stellan, drawn by the gravity in Bear's voice. "What's happening. You know something?"

"I make it my business to know. As a healer I try to find where spirits are disturbed. Help them find peace and rest. But rich people these days are fucking that up."

"And yet they feel oppressed." Asher said.

"They always do. They feel that if they do not have something a poor man has, then it is unfair to them. The ones who have it all."

"Maybe it's a rich asshole that's messing with things."

"When is it not? The very earth beneath us holds power," Bear continued, his fingers tracing invisible patterns on the worn wooden table. "Power that some seek to exploit, heedless of the consequences."

Asher nodded as he was finding common ground with Bear, "And the coyotes? The helicopter? How do they fit into this?" He was trying to rush to get to the finish. He did not understand that Bear was already explaining everything to him.

Bear's face remained as serious. It was hard to read what was going through his head. Normally Stellan had a talent for this. It's what helped him be a MP for the last several years. Bear was a vault of knowledge and a defense that was unbeatable. Stellan knew he would hate playing poker with Bear. The man could probably have a two and a joker card and make you think he had a full house.

"You have a big problem. The coyotes…" Bear began to get into it now. "I could smell their scent, but it is not coyote."

"Then what is it?" Stellan asked. Hoping very much this was heading to another joke. Maybe Bear was just that cool.

"It is the scent of a yee naaldlooshii"

"The fuck is that?" Asher asked.

"Today it is called a skinwalker. It is when someone of my people commit taboos to acquire the power to shift. This allows them to take form of any animal of their choosing. We healers and others refer to them as witches. For they are no longer part of any tribe. They have turned their backs to the traditions and nature."

"Shape shifters?" Stellan asked.

"Yes, but not what you see in the movies."

"What about werewolves?"

"No not like that either. Though many try to associate the two together. Growing up skinwalkers were told as stories that were similar or werewolves where the storyteller simply implied the two could be exchanged equally. They are not."

"So, what is it? If it's not like a werewolf."

"Depends on the one who committed the taboos. Mostly skinwalkers do not hunt people. The only true victim is a loved one who was sacrificed in the ritual."

"They murdered someone?"

Bear nodded as he did not like the idea of a fellow Native doing so. "They do this so they can change into to an animal. To travel great distances, to escape, or hide. Other times it is to seek revenge against foes, which is actually a rare thing."

"The coyotes we saw the other night could have easily killed us. But I feel they were just trying to scare us." Stellan explained.

"Did you flee?"

"We got the hell out of there."

"Then it worked. They only kill when it is the last resort. My advice is to stay away from the area you encountered them. They have thinking skills of a man, but not the reasoning. It is why this is greatly discouraged. The longer you stay an animal, the more you lose what makes you human." Bear explained.

"I get that. I get that skinwalkers are real, as hard as it is to believe." Asher said under his breath. But if they are territorial. Then why are they not attacking those guys that own the helicopters?

"That is quite strange. Most likely these skinwalkers are tied to them. It is strange that somone may have power over them or it could be something simple. Like a mutual benefit to them being in their domain."

"Who are these men then? What are digging for?" Stellan asked hoping Bear could shed light on them.

"If they dare dig in the land of the skinwalkers. Then they are evil men seeking to seize power. There is no other reason a man would tread where they do not belong."

"I'll say." Asher added. "A guard of these guys said we pissed off a coven."

"You said nothing of a coven."

"Is that bad?"

"Oh yes." Bear replied uneasely. Stellan hated how Bear's voice seemed to be more alarmed now. "A coven can only mean one thing." Bear paused and polished off the fireball. "You have many witches to worry about and those witches have control over the skinwalkers. You are fortunate to be living now. Heed my warning. Once they see you as a threat, they will come for you. Seeing you are alive means they are focusing on something else."

"The thing they're digging up?" Asher made the connection.

"That is all I have for you."

***

Stellan felt a chill run down his spine, the weight of Bear's warning settling over him like a shroud. He pushed open the heavy wooden door of the Sleepy Deer, the cool night air hitting him like a slap to the face. His mind buzzed with Bear's warnings, each word seeming to carry the weight of centuries. Asher followed close behind, his usual swagger replaced by an uncharacteristic silence.

"What do you make of all that?" Stellan asked, as they stepped into their jeep.

Asher ran a hand through his hair, frustration evident in every movement. "I don't know, man. Sounds like a load of mystical bullshit to me. But..." He trailed off, his eyes scanning the darkness around them. He was looking for the right words, but they were too distant from him.

Stellan nodded, understanding his friend's conflicted thoughts. "But it fits, doesn't it? The coyotes, those guys, this whole damn mess."

Stellan started the jeep. He didn't know what to tell Asher. He didn't even know what to do. This so-called covenant was digging something up and now he and Asher may be a couple of loose ends that needed to be tied up. He could feel what Bear said was true. It would only be a short time until this covenant would turn its attention on them. At least they had some time, but he didn't know how much.

They were about to take off when they felt something heavy hit the back seat of their jeep. Stellan and Asher looked at one another. They were sharing the same thought. Neither of them wanted to admit it, but they both believed a skinwalker just jumped into the backseat of their jeep.

35

They whirled around to find Bear, somehow having materialized inside the vehicle. Without a word, he climbed into the back seat, settling in as if he'd been invited along.

Stellan blinked, momentarily stunned. "Uh, Bear... what are you doing?"

"We are friends now."

"Yeah," Asher chimed in, finding his voice. "We appreciate the info, but we've got to head back to base."

Bear's face remained unfazed and expressionless. "You will be happy to have me company."

Stellan exchanged a glance with Asher, seeing his own confusion mirrored there. "Look," Stellan tried again, "we don't have a place for you, and there's no time to make arrangements."

"We're not allowed to bring guest to the base either."

"I know," Bear replied, his tone maddeningly calm. He made no move to leave the jeep.

Stellan felt a headache coming on. He looked at Asher, who shrugged helplessly. The absurdity of the situation hit him, and he had to stifle a laugh. Here they were, two trained soldiers, completely at a loss on how to handle this.

"Fine," Stellan sighed.

The jeep drove away from the Sleepy Deer. Stellan and Asher said nothing during the trip back to El Paso. Stellan would check the mirror. Bear's face illuminated by the dim interior lights of the vehicle. Bear never said anything. He just sat back there and looked forward with his stoic look. Stellan focused on the road.

CHAPTER 4

Stellan's fingers flew across the keyboard, his jaw clenched tight enough to crack walnuts as breathes of frustration escaped his lips. The glare from the laptop screen began to burn his eyes with each article he dug into; furrowing his brow. He'd been at this for hours, chasing digital ghosts through a quagmire of dead ends and firewalls.

"How do tin-hats do it?" he muttered, eyes scanning another useless corporate website. "Data on this. Data on that and it all goes no where!" He threw up his hands in despair.

But Clover Security and Defense might as well have been a black hole, swallowing up every scrap of intel he tried to dig up. Stellan's military training had taught him persistence, but this was like trying to scale a sheer cliff with his bare hands.

He took in a deep breath and exhaled loudly through his nose as he flicked the wheel of his mouse. With a defeated glance he caught sight of a link. His frustration began to turn to curiosity as he clicked on it. A grainy photo of a man with cold eyes and an arrogant smirk. Stellan read the caption: Theodore Whelham Pikeman.

"Figures I'd be looking for a smug son of a bitch." Stellan growled, diving deeper into the article. The words painted a damning picture – allegations of kickbacks, hush money, a trail of conveniently silenced whistleblowers. All neatly swept under the rug.

"What makes you so special that you can break the rules?"

Across the room, Asher's voice cut through Stellan's concentration. His tone was smooth as polished steel, but Stellan could hear the underlying tension.

"I appreciate your time, ma'am. But you know who I can talk to about Clover?"

A pause, Asher's fingers drumming an impatient rhythm on the desk.

"It's fine. I was just curious about 'em is all."

Stellan glanced up, catching the flash of frustration on his friend's face. Asher's dropped his head as he listened to the voice on the other end of the line.

"Of course. I never called and you never talked to me. Thank you."

Another pause, longer this time. Stellan watched Asher's knuckles whiten as he gripped the phone.

Asher set the phone down with exaggerated care, like he was fighting the urge to hurl it across the room. He met Stellan's questioning gaze and shook his head.

"Just who the hell are these guys? They got everyone scared of them."

Stellan leaned back, rubbing his eyes. "What are they saying?"

Asher's gave out a sarcastic laugh. "Oh they had plenty to say in we need to back off." Asher turned and made a polite gesture. "In a nice way."

"Of course!" Stellan laughed.

"They just talked mostly about weird ghosts stories and boogey men. You hear a bump in the night? Whatever made it probably works for them."

A chill crept down Stellan's spine. Sounded like the articles about Clover was all real. Vague articles, quiet witnesses and/or victims. It was clear this company was the type who didn't like loose ends.

"What about you?" Asher asked.

"Pretty much the same thing but written. You find tons on Clover, but it says nothing." His partner's eyes were haunted. "I don't know, man."

Stellan's fingers drummed a restless rhythm on the desk. "Pikeman's history is a minefield, Asher. Embezzlement accusations, whispers of arms dealing... but nothing ever sticks. It's like he's got some kind of Teflon coating."

"At least you found out something. Sounds like a scapegoat, but better than nothing."

"I guess. Just garbage. He sounds like every other CEO of a major company. A bunch of scandals, but has friends everywhere who owes him favors out the ass. There's nothing he can't get away with."

"Maybe he should run for president."
Stellan snorted. Wouldn't be the first time some a-hole with money took over.

Asher rolled his eyes. He voice became more intense. "And CSD? They're not just your average security outfit. Pikeman sounds like a middle guy."

"I'm sure that's all he is. What I want to know what he's got us in the middle of."

"I mean we can drop it anytime." Asher reminded Stellan that this was really just a personal project for them.

Stellan sat quietly. He wasn't going to walk away. He did not like the CSD being close to home.

Stellan's blue eyes narrowed, a muscle twitching in his jaw. "We're missing something big here." He broke the silence. :These bastards are operating right under our noses, and nobody's willing to talk."

"Or able to," Asher added, his usual confidence tinged with unease.

A heavy silence fell between them, only the distant hum of the office could be heard. Stellan's mind raced, piecing together fragments of a puzzle that seemed to grow more ominous by the second.

"We keep digging," Stellan finally said, his voice steeled with determination. "Nah, I really want to know what they're doing."

"I be lying if I said I didn't either." And the two laughed once more.
The sharp rap on their office door made both men jump. Sergeant Reeves' gruff voice cut through air. "Ward, Martinez."

Stellan and Asher stood at attention as their commanding officer entered the room. The sergeant's broad shoulders were rigid, his pace brisk. Stellan's combat-honed instincts screamed danger.

Reeves closed the door behind him, his weathered face etched with concern.

"I know you guys been working on that case file with the hiker. I thought you might want to know his name was Romero Gomez," Reeves said, his voice unnaturally flat. "Our dead hiker was an ATF agent, undercover division."

"ATF?"

"Yeah and the commander is wondering why he was found dead on our grounds."

"All we know it might have a connection with the CSD." Stellan answered.

"CSD?"

"Clover Security and Defense company."

"Sounds like another damn military contract company."

"It is." Asher replied.

"Well what are they doing that involves a dead ATF."

"We don't know, sir."

"Well get back to it. I want a report before you shove off to Iraq. Sooner this is wrapped up I can get back to important shit."

"Yes, sir." Both Asher and Stellan said in unison.

"Dismissed." And with that their sergeant exited the office.

Asher and Stellan walked over to the coffee pot. Asher was first to pour. "I mean a dead ATF? Not like that's weird around El Paso."

"True. But at least that might give us something to work with."

"I guess I'll be making a different call now." Asher said sensing what Stellan was going to ask next.

"I knew you were a cool guy!" Stellan laughed and slapped Asher on the back.

***

Overall the day felt waisted. Stellan learned all he could about Pikeman, but the CSD was just as untouchable as before. Asher was able to get ahold of a series of people about Gomez, but still nothing that could be linked to the CSD. How could a major company exist and not have any evidence of its existence.

"Alright." Asher finally said. "I'm done being a ghostbuster for a day."

"Want to get a drink? I know I could use one."

"I say go visit Abigail and your kid. She probably misses you."

"I think Lauren would be glad you're out of the house for a while."

The phone rang and Asher checked the caller ID and saw it read Lauren Martinez.

"Oh look! She misses me, even called to check on me." He laughed.

Before Stellan could respond, the color of his friend's face drained he answered.

"Lauren? Slow down—what's wrong?"

Stellan's heart rate spiked. The panic in Asher's voice was unmistakable.

"We're coming! Right now! Lock the doors, stay away from windows. Grab the gun and wait for me in the bathroom." He quickly instructed. "I love you too."

Asher's hands shook as he slammed the phone on the hook. "Some bastard just threatened Lauren and Abigail is with her!" Stellan's blood ran cold.

As they rounded the final corner onto Asher's street, Stellan's trained eyes caught movement. A massive black pickup, engine roaring, peeled away from the curb in front of Asher's house.

"There!" Stellan shouted, stomping on the brakes.

Asher's head snapped up. "Son of a bitch! Come on!"

Stellan threw the car into reverse, tires squealing as they spun around to give chase.

Asher was already on his phone. "Lauren? You okay? We're on their asses—yeah, black pickup. Stay inside, we'll be right back."

Stellan's heart pounded as he weaved through terrain, keeping the truck's taillights in view. The loose gravel nearly caused Stellan to lose control, but the jeep stayed true to the road.

The pickup truck barreled down the dirt road, tires screeching as it took a sharp turn. All four wheels spinning in place as the massive truck turned broadside to Stellan and Asher. Stellan gripped the steering wheel, his knuckles white, as he pushed their vehicle to its limits.

"Damn, they're fast," Stellan muttered, his eyes narrowing on the truck ahead. "Any plates?"

Asher leaned forward, squinting. "Can't make it out. They're throwing too much dirt."

Stellan's mind raced, adrenaline coursing through his veins. Both vehicles swerved as they stayed on the path. Stellan prayed that no one else would get on the road. It was already difficult to stay on them.

"Hold on," he warned, as he gunned it again edging closer to the truck. Asher braced himself against the dashboard.

They bumped the truck, causing it crash through a street lamp, knocking it down. It got back to the center. Stellan hit them again. The truck moved lurched forward.

Stellan felt he could take them on and drove as he slammed the accelerator with his foot, but the pickup made a quick cut across the sidewalks across someone's yard. Stellan slammed on the break and made the turn. He lost distance as he rounded the corner.

Asher kept his sights on the pickup. Stellan once again floored it as the jeep's motor roared.

As he got closer, he hated what he could see up ahead. It was I-10, the largese road in El Paso. He cursed as he traced them going up the onramp. Cars were beginning to get in the way. He even watched as they side swiped a car, forcing it to go sideways as an attempt to block them.

Luckily, the unfortunate driver was able to maintain himself. He braked and steadied the car, unknowngly helping Stellan to get by and follow them onto I-10.

Stellan could not believe how a large pickup was able to weave through traffic so elegantly. He speeding faster and faster as Stellan tried to keep up. He nearly hit a car here and there. He ignored the angry honking of the drivers. Slowly, Stellan was making up the distance. He saw the driver was checking his mirrors for them.

"He can't possibly be able to push it harder than he already is." Asher said, trying to make Stellan feel better.

Stellan knew it was true to what Asher was saying, but this mysterious driver knew this went both ways. Stellan was pushing the jeep hard as well. He watched as the needle on the dash was getting cloer to the red. He hoped that the engine would hold out and that guy's wouldn't. But if he was a lucky guy, he wouldn't be in the miltary to begin with. Let alone chasing this jackass down the I-10. Stellan gritted his teeth.

"Focus!" Asher said calmly as he took a glance at Stellan. He could feel Stellan was getting pissed. "This isn't GTA."

"I know! I know!" Stellan snapped back. It didn't bother Asher though. Both knew their emotions were running high.

It felt as though an invisible force was between him and the pickup. It felt like the jeep was dragging something behind and he prayed to God that it wasn't some dumbass kid he had ran over.

The pickup continued to manuever around cars, and each time he was gaining distance over them when they found themselves in between two semi trucks. One pulling a large white trailer, and the other a flatbed of military trucks being shipped to another base somewhere.

"Whatcha going to do now?" Stellan asked with a smile. He had that fucker now.

What happened next took Stellan by surprise. As the pickup edged to the front of these road behemoths, he cut the white trailer truck off and hit his brakes. The driver, instintively slammed on the breaks as he cussed in his hispanic tongue.

He swirved to miss the pickup, but the driver veered in the same direction. He lead the truck into the other. The military driver saw what was happening and slammed on his brakes as well as he tried to swirve to the left to avoid the collision.

The mysterious driver gunned his pickup and shot forward in time. The military truck hit the barrier as the white trailer truck hit the side of him. Stellan slammed on the brakes and came to a stop with the trucks. Cars behind the trucks smashed into the trailers. Other cars into them. Stellan looked back to see the cars piling up.

He and Asher looked forward, and saw in the far distance, their man taking the first exit and disappearing from sight.

"Damn it to hell!" Stellan said as he slapped the steering wheel on the side.

***

It took hours to get out of that jam. Once the tow trucks arrived and separated the two semis, Stellan was free to move. The officer waved him out and they took the first exit off of I-10. Their guy was gone and there was no way they were going to find him now.

"Double back to the house!" Asher said. "I need to see Lauren." Stellan nodded and nearly tipped the jeep as he made a Uturn. His knuckles turned white as he gripped the steering wheel.

The jeep came to a screeching halt in front of Lauren's house. His eyes darted across the front yard, scanning for any signs of danger. Asher was out before the engine died, sprinting towards the door.

"Lauren!" Asher's voice cracked with desperation as he burst inside.
Stellan followed, his military training kicking in as he and Asher cleared each room. The house was silent, save for a muffled sob from the bathroom.

They found Lauren huddled in a corner, arm wrapped tightly around Abigail. In her other arm was a shotgun ready to blast any monster that came. Her eyes were wide with fear, but relief flooded her face as she saw Asher.

"Thank God," Asher breathed, embracing them both.

Stellan stood guard at the doorway, his mind racing. "Lauren, are you hurt?"
She shook her head, her voice trembling. "No, we're... we're okay. But that man..."
Asher pulled back, cupping her face. "What man? What did he do?"

Lauren took a shaky breath. "He just appeared in the living room. I didn't hear him come in. He... he said to tell you to stop. That this was your final warning."

"He talked about a coven," Abigail whispered, her brow furrowing. "Said you were meddling in things beyond your understanding."

Asher and Stellan exchanged a look, the gravity of the situation sinking in.

"This is insane," Stellan muttered, more to himself than anyone else. "Covens? Disappearing trucks?"

Asher waved his hand at Stellan to calm down. Then directed his attention to Lauren. "I don't know, but they've crossed a line. Threatening our family? That's not something I'm going to let slide."

Stellan nodded, his mind whirling with possibilities. None of it made sense, yet the danger felt more real than anything he'd faced before.

Lauren's voice cut through their thoughts. "Whatever is going on, please make it stop."

The fear in her eyes drove home the stakes. This wasn't just about solving a mystery anymore. It was about protecting the people they loved from a threat they did not understand.

Stellan and Asher looked to one another. The weight of their decision hung in the air, heavy with the gravity of what lay ahead.

"We don't have much time. We need to do something," Asher said, his voice low but resolute.

Stellan nodded, feeling the familiar surge of adrenaline that came before a mission. "I guess we need to find Bear."

"Maybe he has something?"

The darkness seemed to close in around them. Stellan helped Abigail get into her SUV while Lauren got into the driver's seat.

Asher loaded up some suitcases in the back of the vehicle as Stellan guarded the girls. He didn't say anything, but he had the feeling feeling of being watched. He knew what it was. It was the skinwalkers. They were watching what he did. He didn't understand why they didn't attack. He, Asher, and the girls were out in the open. But they stayed back. He thought he saw an outline of a coyote, but it could had been his eyes playing tricks on him. Because why not? Everything else has.

45

CHAPTER 5

The aroma of stale coffee and greasy burgers hung in the air of the diner. Stellan's fingers drummed as he conversed with Asher. They spoke quietly about what they had gathered so far. Stellan would stop his anxious rhythm on the tabletop and begin again after as his eyes darted between the clock on the wall and the dinner's entrance. An hour had crawled by each minute stretching like taffy in the oppressive desert heat.

"He's not coming," Asher finally muttered, voicing the fear gnawing at Stellan's gut. "I knew we couldn't count on him."

Stellan opened his mouth to respond when Stellan spotted Bear sitting on the other side of the room. Stellan palmed Asher's head and turned it to Bear's direction.

"Damn it. Has he been here the whole time?"

Stellan rolled his eyes, and they walked over to Bear's table. They sat down across from him. "We've been waiting for an hour."

"So have I."

"Why didn't you say you were here?" Asher asked.

"You two looked like you were having an important conversation. I did not want to be rude."

"Never mind." Stellan replied. He felt this could go on forever. "Where have you been?"

Bear began, " Around, but there is not much to be found. Your enemies have a way of disappearing."

"You have no idea." Asher said, remembering last night car chase that turned into a ghost chase.

Bear began again, his dark eyes holding a depth that made Stellan wonder if he was seeing more than just the physical world. "I went to the Outpost. Only empty buildings, mostly. But there I found someone had been there and traces of Peyote."

"Traces of what?" Asher leaned forward, eager for information.

"Peyote," Bear replied, his voice dropping to barely above a whisper. "And San Pedro Cacti. Plants my people use for rituals."

Stellan's mind raced. He did not want to hear about rituals. "What would they use these plants for?"

Bear's expression darkened. "These plants were used in our rituals for generations. A way to connect with the spirit world, to gain wisdom and healing." His fingers traced patterns on the table's surface, as if drawing invisible sigils. "Until your government decided to ban peyote in '70s because it was being abused for its hallucinogens."

"You think the CSD is running drugs."

"No, I don't. They got enough money, and I didn't see anything drug related when I was digging on them." Stellan explained.

"Another dead end?"

"Maybe so," Stellan murmured, more to himself than the others. He looked up at Bear, searching for any sign that he had more. But all he saw was a man carrying the weight of centuries of oppression and lost traditions.

As Bear nodded solemnly.

"Well before it was banned, what could it be used for."

"Medicine." Bear began to explain. "Some of your doctors were using it to research rheumatism."

Stellan and Asher reflected on that bit of information. Asher then broke their concentration, "Isn't there a major pharmaceutical company down over here?"

Bear reached into his worn leather satchel, pulling out a stack of documents and maps. "I was able to get these." He said, his voice low.

"How?"

"I have a way with computers."

"You mean you hacked them or something?" Stellan asked with a smile spreading across his face.

"Not really. I have been taught ways of searching for things on the internet. It is about how you search for things. I find it like finding trails that are digital as the ones that are physical in our world."

Stellan's brow furrowed as he took the papers, his fingers tracing the edges carefully. He spread them out on the table, eyes scanning methodically over each detail. His jaw clenched as he absorbed the information, piecing together fragments of a puzzle that made his skin crawl.

Asher leaned in, his gaze sharp. "Wait, I recognize this," he said, tapping a photograph. "That's the old Whalstraus research facility. Abandoned years ago, but..." He trailed off, a spark of realization in his eyes.

Stellan's mind raced. "Well, if they're working with the government, they probably left a lot of shit there."

"Close enough for government work, right?" Asher laughed.

Bear nodded; his expression unreadable. "Take me there and we can maybe find out more about them."

"I was thinking the same way." Stellan replied, already mentally cataloging the gear they'd need.

He pictured the facility, imagining shadows watching him. Time was running out and he would soon be on the other side of the world. He knew they needed to start working this at a faster pace.
***

The abandoned Whalstraus research facility loomed before them, a hulking silhouette against the starlit sky. Stellan's breath caught in his throat as he took in the ominous structure. Its appearance was evidence of neglect. Its broken windows like empty eye sockets staring into the night. The silence was oppressive, broken only by the whisper of wind through overgrown weeds.

"Christ," Asher muttered beside him. "This place gives me the creeps."

"I was hoping it was in better shape." Bear added.

Stellan nodded, his hand instinctively moving to check his sidearm. "Stay sharp. We don't know what we're walking into."

"If anything, listen to your surroundings. Places of evil such as this can deceive your eyes. Trust your ears." Bear explained.

Stellan and Asher helped Bear with the specialized equipment he'd brought with him.

"So how you learn about all this?" Asher asked Bear.

"The university. Go Miners."

"Wait!" Stellan said as he turned around to Bear. "Are you telling me you have a college degree?"

"Yes. In computer science. Thought it would be useful as the world seems to be doing this digital thing."

"How did you afford college?" Asher asked. "I'm sorry that sounded rude." Asher apologized. "I didn't mean to make it sound you were poor."

"First white men take my land. Then white men say my gods not good enough. Then you believe me to be uneducated." Bear said sternly.

"I... I..." Asher turned red.

"I'm fucking with you again." Bear said flatly as he had done before. "I got scholarship because my land was stolen. I guess it makes us even somehow?" Bear paused to think about it. "I guess in a manifest destiny kind of way."

"You..." Stellan began to ask.

"Got a minor in history." Bear explained further.

Now, standing before the facility's rusted entrance, Stellan felt the weight of that equipment in his backpack. He turned to Asher, keeping his voice low. "Remember the plan. We get in, find a secure spot to set up, and get out."

Asher nodded; he knew they were taking a risk being here. "You got it."

Stellan pushed open the door, wincing at the loud creak that echoed through the empty corridors. They stepped inside, the beam of their flashlights cutting through the darkness. Dust motes danced in the light, and the musty smell of abandonment filled Stellan's senses and his anxiety.

As they moved deeper into the facility, Stellan was on high alert. Every shadow seemed to hold a potential threat, every distant sound a warning. They scanned each room they passed, noting the toppled furniture and scattered papers.

"This place is a maze," Asher whispered, frustration in his voice. "How the hell are we supposed to find anything useful?"

Stellan paused, but before he answered, Bear said. "We are not here to find physical evidence. We just need to set up the equipment. This location was only recently abandoned. The power still runs through. We may be able to look into their digital vault."

They pressed on, navigating the labyrinthine corridors. Stellan's mind raced, cataloging possible escape routes. He knew if they got into trouble, there was no way to fight the CSD or if they sick their Skinwalkers on them. Which they may do. The feeling made Stellan feel unease.

What if we're in over our heads? he thought. What if CSD is more than we can handle?

He pushed the doubts aside, focusing on the task at hand. They were already beyond the point of no return. Whatever secrets this facility held, whatever truths lay hidden in CSD's network, they were going to discover them if they wanted to or not.

***

Bear's eyes narrowed as he spotted a promising room ahead. "There," he whispered, gesturing to Asher. "That looks secure enough."

The room was small, windowless, with a heavy metal door. Perfect for their needs. Stellan quickly swept the area, checking for any hidden dangers or surveillance equipment.

"All clear," he said, his voice low. "Let's get set up."

Asher nodded, pulling out the equipment Bear had provided. Stellan's hands moved with practiced efficiency, connecting wires, and powering up devices. His mind, however, was racing.

"I've got your six," Asher murmured, positioning himself near the door. His eyes scanned the hallway, alert for any sign of trouble.

Bear plugged the Ethernet cord into the socket and into the port of his computer. He calmly reached into his pocket and pulled out a piece of paper. On it read something unusual, but to Bear it made sense as he opened the CMD and began typing on it. A whole lot of other stuff began to happen that made no sense to Asher and Stellan. It looked nothing like the movies, it just looked like Bear was using the computer like anyone else. To be honest, they were very disappointed.

Bear sensed the two had been watching him, and saw their disappointment and said, "I'm in." Which brought a smile to both Stellan and Asher's face. He followed along the sign Suddenly, the screen lit up with a login prompt. He typed 'PASSWORD' and hit enter, half-expecting it to fail. To his shock, though his facial expression remained unchanged, the system accepted it immediately.

"You've got to be kidding me," Asher said, glancing over his shoulder. "That actually worked?"

"Passwords and digital gatekeeping do not seem to be a concern for white men, Warrior."

Bear found his way to the server. He followed through the documents. Mostly finding payrolls, but those only had numbers. Countless excel sheets, memos, and other things such as birthday parties planned. Nothing really seems to open for them. "How much time do we have?" Asher asked, his voice tight with tension.

Stellan checked his watch. "I don't know. I've never done this before."

"It will not be too long for their cybersecurity team to find us. We are using a port that should have been terminated a long time ago. Our IP address will be found soon."

"Keep looking for anything." Stellan told him. "We'll worry about the fall out later."

Bear plugged a flash drive into the other port of the computer. He had it ready for him to download anything.

They worked in tense silence; it looked like a wild goose chase when Bear came across a strange file. To Stellan and Asher, it looked normal, but what stood out to Bear was it was a file that titled RECIEPTS* Bear had recalled that he came across a file with the same name, but the asterisk made it stand out. He opened it and found several files with long numeric titles. When he opened on it was filled with other files and more in there.

"Strange." Was all Bear said.

"What's up?"

Bear said nothing as he continued until he found that there were several documents. Buried in a series of dummy files to fool anyone looking for anything. He quickly began to copy the files to his flash drive. Thank God Bill Gates was wrong about computer memory, and he had a 128MB to play with.

The bar showing the status appeared and everything seemed normal until the CMD prompt window began to flash on and off the screen.

"I think they found us." Bear explained as he watched the status window continue.

"What are they doing?"

"They are looking for our IP Address and MAC ID. I have been using a VPN to make it look like we are somewhere else. But they will soon find us." Bear explained.

Asher and Stellan watched as the status bar came to a crawl. First it said two minutes remaining. Then they gasped when the time went to ten hours.

"Relax." Bear said trying to ease their nerves. "Time is usually inaccurate. Pay attention to the bar. It is nearly done."

As Bear finished his sentence the bar was gone, and he pulled the drive out with the computer warning him that doing so may damage the drive. But everyone ignores it. Just big talk from the CPU. He immediately unplugged the Ethernet cord from the laptop port.

"Thank God!" Asher exclaimed.

"Did they find us."

The facilities lights turned on in a red hue as an alarm was raised.

"I think so." Bear said with no hint of urgency or panic in his voice. "We should go."

Asher, Stellan, and Bear worked fast to pack up their things. When the last bag was zipped up, they could hear a coyote yipping. Followed by another, and another. The haunting chorus of coyotes echoed through the abandoned laboratory, sending a chill down Stellan's spine.

"Skinwalkers are coming." Bear growled, his eyes narrowing as he scanned the darkness.

Stellan's heart hammered in his chest. "Time to leave."

They moved with practiced efficiency, the air thick with unspoken fear. Stellan's mind raced. He wondered what all Bear had found.

The yipping grew closer, more frenzied. Stellan's hand instinctively reached for a weapon that wasn't there. Damn it, he thought. We're sitting ducks.

They hurried through the darkened corridors, Bear leading the way, his massive form a comforting presence in the gloom. Stellan brought up the rear, every shadow seeming to hide a threat.

As they turned a corner, a large coyote stood before them. Teeth barring at them its feet poised and ready to leap. Stellan took a step back ready to pull his pistol, doubting he would be able to hurt it. But damnit, today might be his lucky day.

The coyote though, called him on his bluff as it took a step closer to him. Stellan felt that today was the day the Skinwalkers will kill them rather than scare them off like last time.

Stellan, ready to pull his gun, was beat to the punch when Bear pushed him back. "Stand back, Solider!" Bear commanded as he pulled a small bag from his belt. With precise accuracy, Bear threw the bag at the coyote. It exploded on impact on its nose. Greenish-yellow dust took the air as the scent of sage filled the hallway.

The coyote howled and cried as it shook its head silently. As it rolled on the floor it began to lose its concentration as a man began to form before the group. Stellan and Asher looked on in amazement as they saw a Native American dressed as if he was still in the 1800s.

"Come on! It will not stop him for long." Bear said as he continued to run.

Stellan and Asher ran with him.

"What was that stuff?" Asher asked.

"Sage mostly with other herbs and spices. A Skinwalker adopts both strength and weaknesses of the animals they form into." Bear said as they busted through the exit.

Once outside, they piled into their vehicles, engines roaring to life. In the distance they could see large black pickup trucks and cars driving their way. Stellan quickly put the jeep into gear and sped away.

Miles down the road and no CSD trucks in view or Skinwalkers, Bear pats Stellan on the shoulder. "Let me out here, Soldier boy."

Stellan stops the Jeep and Bear climbed out. "What are you doing?" Stellan looked around for the enemy. "This isn't really a safe place."

"From what I have seen and read today. I can see we are going to need additional help. I am going to contact a friend of mine."

"Who's your friend?" Asher asked.

Bear said nothing and calmly walked away as if the danger they narrowly avoided didn't happen. Stellan watched him as he faded away into nothingness.

"I really wished we hadn't gone camping." Stellan said as they drove away.

CHAPTER 6

Stellan's hands trembled as he spread the damning photos across his worn kitchen table. Each photo, article, snippet of CSD weighed ominously in his hand. In the last couple of days, everything he thought he knew about the world was turning upside down. He could not believe something like the CSD existed or was allowed to exist in his world. Let alone in his own country.

"Jesus, Asher. Are you getting all of this?" Stellan had to push his words out from his lungs. Nervously tapping on a photo of CSD's upside down clover logo. The things he was reading seemed unreal. Sure, he had heard stories, but this came from the company's servers. This was shit they were really pulling right here; right now. He didn't know how this was all possible. "The manpower and the money alone…" he couldn't think of anything else to ask. Anything else to say.

Asher leaned in; his brow furrowed. "I don't want to believe it. But we've seen it." He picked up a memo that had been redacted and scanned. Only to be reprinted. Could this even be permissible in court? Would the court believe it? Or are they part of this? Asher couldn't think who in the government would not be part of this.

Stellan rubbed the back of his head and looked disparagingly into his empty mug for more of that soothing black, reinforced with some peppermint schnapps. But alas it was empty.

Abigail stood in the doorway, her face pale. "Stellan, what's going on? She asked as her as Lauren appeared behind her.

"Someone take a shit your cereal, Asher?" She laughed.

Stellan's chest tightened as he looked to Abigail and his unborn kid. He'd wanted to keep them out of this, to shield them from the danger. He had wished this was open and shut. He just wanted to know what the hell happened on a camping trip. He didn't set out to save the world. Was this what Pandora felt when she opened the box? If so, where was that name spark of hope that was supposed to be in the corner?

Asher got up and stretched and helped Lauren with her bags. It was only a couple of days until they shipped off. And he was nowhere near putting this away. All he had was a couple of documents, some pictures that looked like they came out of syfy.com and if anything, he just has a damn target on his back and probably Lauren's too.

Asher stepped in, ever the diplomat. "Ladies, I wish I could tell you, but I think the less you know, the better."

"So mysterious…" Abigail rolled her eyes.

"Hey!" Stellan turned to her. "Remember, not too long ago we had a creep messing with you and her." He pointed to Lauren.

"You act like this is all some big conspiracy. Creeps will always knock on the door."

"Not like the ones we seen." Stellan muttered wishing it had only been a one-off thing. Shit, he got natives, monsters, and whatever else there is that's attached to this.

As the women settled at the table, Stellan felt the weight of responsibility settle on his shoulders. He'd sworn to protect his country, but now did he had to protect his country from the government now.

Abigail came and rested her arms around Stellan. "It's going to be okay. I don't know what this is you and Asher are doing. I don't pretend to understand what has you upset… scared even. I just know the man I married will rise above this. Not because of some sacred oath as a soldier, or a calling from God. I know because that is the man your parents raised. You don't quit and you don't back down from what's right."

Stellan felt a moment of pride in his wife's voice. He didn't know how she did it, but he was damn glad she does it. She always… ALWAYS knew what to say. Perhaps this was the hope he had been looking for. Not in pictures or papers or even car chases. The hope was the love he and his wife shared. A love that culminated into what would be their future son. And damn it all if he was going to let a bunch of corporate shadows and villains get in his son's way to the future.

"Damn, girl. You always know what to say." He thought about it. He was no way articulate as she was. But he had a simple way of showing his affection. "Thank you."

***

A loud guttural growl sliced through the peaceful silence, freezing Stellan's mind. His eyes locked with Asher's, both men instantly alert. Stellan whispered, his hand instinctively moving towards his sidearm.

Another sound followed – a scratching, scraping noise that seemed to come from all directions at once. Stellan's mind raced, trying to focus on what he was hearing. It was like a pack of wild animals had suddenly surrounded the house. He knew what had come to his home.

"Skinwalkers," Asher sighed, the word tasting like ash in his mouth. "They've found us."

In an instant, Stellan was moving. "Asher, secure the back. I've got the front." His voice was clipped, efficient. "Abigail, Lauren – away from the windows, now!"

As he rushed to bolt the front door, Stellan's mind racing. He tried to remember all points of entry to the house. He had trouble focusing his thoughts as the animals began to howl outside the house. He was prepared in the battlefield, not in his literal home. This can't be happening. Skinwalkers aren't supposed to be real. But the sounds outside gave to the contrary.

"Had to be that asshole from the other night!" Asher called from the kitchen; the sound of a shotgun being racked punctuating his question.

Stellan positioned himself by the living room window, the AR-15 he bought to celebrate his enlistment at the ready. He heard Asher, but he couldn't translate what he was saying. He heard something big romping around outside. Something bigger than a coyote. What else are these assholes capable of? Stellan's finger trembled slightly on the trigger as shadows moved in the darkness beyond the glass.

"What do we do?" Abigail asked. Stellan turned and saw her cocking a pistol and Lauren adjusting her deer rifle.

57

"Lauren! Get something in front of the windows. If something comes through, it needs to slow it down for a good shot. Abigail…" He thought what a woman a couple months pregnant could do in this situation. "Just cover Lauren the best you can."

Lauren shoved the couch next to the window. A window breaking in the kitchen caused them all to stop and turn.

"I'm fine!" Asher called out immediately, so no one panicked. "It's a small window! They're just looking for now."

A loud snort came from the other side of the window. It was the heavy thing Stellan had heard earlier and he knew exactly was it was. They brought a bear to the fight?

Just as Stellan realized it, a massive grizzly bear, its form shimmering and distorting unnaturally, charged the front door. "Jesus Christ!" Stellan yelled. It was like getting hit by a truck. He fell to the floor. The door threatened to be smashed open, but miraculously it held true. Stellan didn't know if it could withstand another brutal assault.

The back of the house in the kitchen did not fare so well. Asher held the kitchen table against the backdoor as hard as he could. There was a sound of a roaring grizzly shoving itself against the door. Its claw had busted through and blindly swiped at Asher. He fired his pistol, but the bear remained unaffected.

"Stellan!" Asher's voice carried from the kitchen. "They're everywhere!"

The bear momentarily backed away. Stellan took his chance to steady himself and couple of shots from his AR-15. He looked out into the yard to see if he had gotten lucky.

For a minute, his fear turned to curiosity as he watched a stark coyote walking on his hind legs. He stretched up and for a moment turned back into a human. He watched as he pulled a feather from a pouch and tuck it into his hair. He expanded his arms out and fell forward. It was like watching a fairy tale as the human transformed into a golden eagle. His wingspan easily ten feet across, slammed against the remaining front windows. His sharp and elongated beak pecked furiously at the glass.

Stellan shook his head as Abigail and Lauren began firing at the bird. "Abigail!" Stellan started his next order. When the front door busted down on top of him under an immense weight, as the massive grizzly bear threw itself against it.

At the same time the back door broke open. Asher fell back and scooted across the floor to the living room.

"We got a breach!" Asher yelled as he picked himself up. He investigated the kitchen and saw a Kodiak bear swiping the table to the side. It was unreal watching the table shatter against the wall.

"A little help?" Stellan called out as he lay under the front door. The grizzly hopped up and down on it, trying to crush him to death.

Asher's eyes widened in panic. He took a couple of shots at the bear, but there was no effect. Asher watched as the bullets hit their mark. Fur and skin departed but grew back instantly as the damage was done.

"Get the girls and run!" Stellan shouted. The window gave in, and the eagle came in screeching. Abigail fell to the floor as Lauren took aim and fired at it. "ABIGAIL!" Stellan shouted as he tried to crawl out from under the battered door. The grizzly took a swipe at him. Stellan barely tilted his head away, feeling not only a close call from the claws but the very feeling of death's touch.

Asher helped Abigail up and pulled Lauren to him. The eagle turned and landed on the window's seal. A couple coyotes jumped through and bared their teeth at them. Asher turned towards the back, but the Kodiak huffed at him. He was trapped as the grizzly bear opened his jaws and descended on Stellan. It was all over now.

The feeling of the end overcame them. Asher dropped his gun and Lauren lowered her rifle.

"Fuck me." Stellan said as he closed his eyes and waited for darkness to take him away from this nightmare. Only if though. He wished with every fiber in his body he would wake up in his tent and this would all be over.

"Stand back!" Bear's powerful command brought silence and all movement to a stop. As his deep voice cut through the pandemonium. He began to chant in a language Stellan didn't recognize, waving the smoking bundle in intricate patterns.

To Stellan's astonishment, the grizzly snorted and shook his head. He was agitated but defenseless as it backed off Stellan. It growled hopelessly at Bear, unable to see him and only bit at the air. Bear remained resilient and unafraid. He never took a step back but moved forward.

"What the hell?" Stellan whispered, unable to believe his eyes. He glanced at Bear, noting the man's calm demeanor amidst the chaos. How can he be so collected right now?

Bear continued his chant, moving forward with steady steps. The smoke from the herbs seemed to coil around the creatures, driving them back. The eagle and coyotes exited through the shattered window. The Kodiak growled in protest but turned away from the smoke and walked out of the door.

"Soldier," Bear said, his tone deadpan despite the intensity of the situation. "See to Warrior and the others. There may still be danger."

Snapping out of his daze, Stellan rushed to help Asher, who had dropped to his knee. As he pulled his friend back to his feet, he couldn't help but ask, "How did you do this?"

Bear's lips twitched in what might have been the ghost of a smile. "I'm a healer."

Then a weathered figure emerged from the shadows behind Bear. He watched as Bear continued his magic. Calmness and peace began to retake the room. The sound of unnatural animals began to fade. The skinwalkers were in full retreat.

"What the actual hell?" Asher asked.

"You fight what is hurting with anger and aggression." Bear explained. "Skinwalkers cannot be hurt, Warrior. You can only heal them."

"If it's healing them, then why do they run away?"

Bear continued his chant and then paused to look around. When he felt confident the Skinwalkers had completely retreated he turned to Asher. "The minds of Skinwalkers are often clouded. I clear their minds and bring their true nature back. It frightens them and they try to run."

"Where?" Abigail asked.

"They run to their tribe to find forgiveness for their foolish acts of taboo. It is most unfortunate though. Their tribe is long gone from this realm. They are running to ghosts who cannot hear them…

or forgive them." Abigail could hear the sadness in the stoic man's voice. This too made her feel sorrow for the Skinwalkers.

"And who the hell is that?" Stellan asked, as a rough looking man had suddenly appeared at their doorsteps. You could tell he had been through it for years. First thoughts of everyone has of a Veteran is usually they're suffering from homelessness or mental health issues.

The old soldier nodded curtly; his steely gaze fixed on the retreating creatures. In his gnarled hands, he clutched a pouch that emanated a pungent aroma. Stellan and Asher could tell by the man's stance he was a former soldier. His age may have gotten the better of his posture but his five o' clock shadow gave the rest away.

"I heard you meddlin' kids been getting your asses kicked." he grunted, his voice gruff but steady. He moved himself at Bear's flank. "The name's Damian."

"Is there a first name on top of that?" Asher asked.

"Damian is all you get. If you're tired of getting the shit kicked out of ya, I suggest you all come with me. I got a place not too far from here and I can maybe give all ya whatcha need."

Stellan's gaze swept across the wreckage of his living room, lingering on the splintered door frame and shattered windows. The acrid smell of gunpowder hung in the air, mingling with the earthy scent of Bear's herbs. His mind struggled to process what he'd just witnessed.

"This is twice Bear's come through for us." Stellan nodded. "He doesn't come across as anyone who trusts people easily."

"So, ya'll comin' or what?" Damian huffed. His patience was running out. He didn't have to prove himself to a bunch of kids and he was aware that Stellan knew that damn well.

"Yes, sir."

"Good, and don't calling me fucking sir!" Damian smiled. Somehow it made him look even more rugged than before. "Get your shit and let's go!"

"I'll gather the papers."

"Forget that. I got what ya need at my place. I've been tracking the CSD for years."

Asher looked to Stellan. Stellan could only shrug and smile. It was a good feeling to have someone who might know a thing or two about the enemy.

CHAPTER 7

The safehouse's dim light told the story of Damian's weathered face as he leaned forward, his voice low and measured. "Clover Security and Defense is one bad mother fucker."

"I know what you mean." Stellan shook his head while Asher nodded.

"No, you don't. You're just agitating them. If they deemed you an actual threat, you'd be gone."

"Listen…" Asher started in. "This isn't a movie. This isn't some Saturday morning villain of the week thing."

"Shut up and listen!" Damian interrupted as he sparked up a cigarette. He offered one to Stellan and Asher, but they had politely declined. "The CSD is a global network. They don't have time with bullshit upstarts Captain America wannabes like you. So far, they tried intimidation tactics. The Native American burial for that ATF guy, the skinwalkers, driving up and knocking on the door."

A chill went down Abigail's back, remembering the truck driver who came to her home. She had been listening to what they were saying. She hoped that all this would come to an end soon.

"They came at you tonight though." Damian continued. "They came at you with magic." He looked over to Bear who was rummaging through the refrigerator. "Good thing you got a healer with you."

Stellan's jaw clenched; his eyes fixed on Damian. The words hit him like rounds of ammunition. He glanced at Asher, noting the slight furrow in his friend's brow, the telltale sign of his skepticism warring with the undeniable weight of Damian's words.

"So, who are these guys?" Asher asked.

"You think it's just a run of the mill security and defense company. Like Black Water or the Wagner Group. These guys been around, and they know how to get around."

63

Stellan chimed in, his voice tight. "United States Contract company?"

"If only!" Damian laughed. "They're in every country. They may have different names, but it's is all the same no matter where you go." Damian took a long drag on his cigarette. Then what little was left went into the ash tray with others. Damian's eyes met Stellan's, a glimmer of respect visible in their depths.

"So, is this a 'want to take over the world' thing?" Stellan asked.

Damian only chuckled some more. "Your friend was right about this not being a Saturday morning villain." He took out another smoke and sparked up again. "They already did it."

"What?" Stellan sat back in his chair.

"Say again?" Asher couldn't believe it.

"They run the show on this blue ball." Damian's grin stretched slowly across this face, stretching his wrinkles, which made him look younger in an unsettling way to Stellan. "They control everything. When someone doesn't play ball, they make sure they strike out. Governments are in the palm of their hands, and they got every politician lining up to lick their sacks."

"But how?"

Asher shifted in his seat; his normally easy demeanor replaced by a tense alertness. "That's a hell of a claim, Damian. You got anything to back that up?"

"Well shit! If I did, you'd and your friend wouldn't be hiding from the big bad wolf, would ya?" Damian smiled and he huffed on his cancer stick. Stellan watched as Damian reached into his jacket, producing a worn leather notebook. The sight of it sent a chill down Stellan's spine. He could feel powerful secrets pulling him in like being on the crevice of a black hole. He wanted to leave, he felt if he came closer to that book, he would be sucked into another world. A world where nothing made sense and the strange and weird ruled where there should have been order.

"I have this though," Damian replied, his fingers tracing the notebook's cover. "I made notes, maps, photographs, sketches, and I even have witness recordings."

"So, what happened?" Stellan had to know.

"Well, it turns out no one wants to do anything about it. Whether they think you're crazy and making shit up for attention. Or they think you're crazy to think you can do anything about it. Or. OR! They just don't care." He opened the notebook but not to any specific page.

As Damian began to recount specific instances of CSD's manipulation. World leaders assassinated, starting rebellions, paying terrorists, intimidation, assaults, disappearances. The list went on and one. One event after another, Stellan felt his world tilting on its axis. Everything he thought he knew, everything he'd fought for – it was all being called into question.

His mind raced. Remembering stories from veterans about past missions. Trainings and simulated situations flickering through his consciousness like a warped slideshow. How much has been orchestrated by CSD? How many lives had been lost in service of this shadowy conspiracy?

"Jesus," Asher muttered, running a hand through his dark hair. "If even half of this is true..."

Stellan nodded, his voice barely above a whisper. "Everything I know. Care about. It's all chainging."

Damian's gaze swept between them, his expression grim. "Trust me, it gets a lot more complicated than that!" He grinned as the end of the cigarette burned to ashes, which fell to the floor. "I haven't even gotten to the good part. All that was just setting up the game board to them!"

Stellan braced himself. He didn't know how much more he could take. He wondered if they would even leave him and Asher alone after hearing this. How did he know they weren't listening now or watching him? Could he even trust anyone after this?

Damian's weathered hands opened the leather-bound notebook again, revealing yellowed pages covered in spidery script. Stellan leaned forward, his eyes straining in the dim light of the safehouse.

"Let me tell you a little story about Alaziah Whalstraus," Damian intoned, his voice dropping to a near whisper. "One of the most dangerous individuals you never heard of."

Stellan felt the hairs on the back of his neck stand up. "Who was she?"

Damian's eyes gleamed with a mixture of fascination and fear. "Not was. She IS a witch. But not just any witch. Alaziah is possessed by something angry and vengeful." As Damian spoke, he pulled out a picture and pushed it across to Stellan and Asher. A woman with raven-black hair and eyes that glowed like embers, standing outside of an airplane. Wind blowing her hair back as she looked far off. Her black lipstick gave her the features of a very young woman.

"God damn, she's beautiful!" Announced Asher. Quickly followed by Lauren clearing her throat. "No seriously! You'd want to leave me for her if you got the chance."

"I'll ignore the implications of that." Lauren replied.

Damian ignored the interruption. "Alaziah's origin is unimportant. What she's doing is."

"So! We find her, arrest her…" Stellan thought about it and put it simply, "what? This ends everything? The world goes back to what I know is right?"

"Wish that could be it. She's just a gear in a clockwork of large machine." Damian answered. Stellan did not like the sound of that.

Stellan's blood ran cold. "Of what?"

"A secret society of dangerous people," Damian explained, his eyes never leaving the page. "Puppet masters pulling strings. They call themselves the Thule Society."

Stellan's mind reeled. Ancient witchcraft and modern corporate espionage? It seemed impossible, and yet...

"How does something like this happen?" he managed to ask.

Damian's gaze met Stellan's, and in that moment, Stellan saw a flicker of genuine fear in the older man's eyes.

"It is because sometimes things in the past want to be alive still. Nature of all things is to survive."

Damian's fingers drummed nervously on the table. "Of course, the Thule Society is paying the Coven."

"Alright, so who's footing in the bill?" Asher asked. Stellan could hear the exhaustion of all this. Secret societies, an immortal witch, skinwalkers. He was sure that if Asher hadn't been part of his personal crusade against this, he'd walk away a long time ago.

Damian could probably sense it too. Stellan studied him as he spoke. There had to been something that had happened to Damian long ago to investigate all this. Perhaps he was mad too and all this is just some coincidental bullshit he stepped into, and Damian is just another nut in the mixture. But he was here and all that happened allowed him to know there was something here. Something bad and if it wasn't trying to kill him, Stellan found himself somewhat in awe and surprised by this underground world.

"There's someone, someone even I cannot possibly understand." His voice dropped to a whisper. "Frankly, he gives me the creeps. Never saw the guy myself. But I know how to find people. Witnesses." He put out the cigarette and his hand found the glass of tequila. Stellan and Asher watched as he took a large gulp. It was as if Damian expected to die after what he was about to tell them. "They call him 'The Chairman'." He then dug into his leather book and pulled out a picture. It was a man dressed well enough to put a businessman of a 500 club to shame. He stood taller than anyone else in the picture. He carried a cane, his hands gloved in gold and silver gauntlets, but it was the fact that he wore a helmet with a face cover that created a mystic fog or eerie to him.

Asher reached for the photo for a better look, but Damian snatched it from him. "This is the only photo I have of him. I have gone through databanks, people, moles. This is the only known photo of him. And it was the last picture my son took before…" he couldn't finish.

Stellan leaned back, heart racing. "Who is he?" But he already had an idea. A ghost from the past that refused to move on. Made his way through the world and he runs the place now. People like him didn't need a name. They didn't need a hype man. They only existed and their presence of the world was known far and wide even if you couldn't understand what was happening. All Stellan knew and needed to know, that this man was the guy who threatened everything he held dear. What made it worse. From what Damian had explained so far, this bastard had no idea that he, Stellan Ward, shared the planet with him.

"That's just it," Damian said, shaking his head. "Nobody knows. Some say he's not even human."

"Don't tell me he's an alien." Stellan huffed. "That would be quite a letdown."

"Please." Damian huffed. "Let's not get crazy here. He's not an alien, they're nice. They're helpful. They love us. This guy is the reason they don't want to be known."

A chill ran down Stellan's spine. He knew that last part was a joke, but he did not dare to laugh. Maybe it was true what Damian said. Maybe it was the atmosphere. Maybe it was all this nonsense that was happening. But Stellan felt deep down that if The Chairman didn't know he existed. Laughing at the joke would have made him aware and he would magically appear and beat the living shit out of him. Stellan nodded and had a drink of his own. The safehouse suddenly felt colder, darker.

"Okay enough of the boogey man." Asher finally made his pitch. "The thing is he doesn't know about us. Otherwise, we would be dead. Also, he's on the other side of the world… maybe… but he isn't here. What is this witch doing and why is the CSD protecting her and her drug company?"

Damian's expression turned grim. "That's why I am here. I keep in contact with Bear a lot of times. He had already knew I was here doing my own thing when I came across you two clowns." He pulled out a small orange pill bottle, setting it on the table with a soft click. "Have you ever heard of MK Ultra?"

"What do you mean clowns?"

"Hell, I was already up to my shitter in this investigation, and I found you two poking a hornet's nest. What the hell did you think you were going to accomplish?"

"Okay! Sorry. I'm new to all this. Anyways what is MK Ultra?" Stellan asked.

"CIA mind control experiments, right? Cold War stuff." Damian leaned back as he sucked more on his cancer stick. Stellan felt that every puff and drag took another day off Damian's life. But he could tell Damian wasn't exactly keen on life now. "It was after World War II, and everyone got into mind control. I'm talking the

Russians, China, and the Germans were already working on it when we adopted them."

"You mean Nazis?"

"That's right. The people Thule bankrolled to take over the world for them."

Stellan stared at the innocuous-looking pill, his mouth dry. "Mind control?"

"In its purest form," Damian confirmed. "One pill, and you're completely under their control. No will of your own, no memories of what you've done. It was formed during the time MK Ultra evolved to become MK Seeker. Thus, was born the Manchurian Project."

"Wait! Like the movie, the Manchurian Candidate? That shit is real?"

Damian nodded.

"Jesus," he muttered. "And CSD has this?"

Damian laughed gravely. "They're manufacturing it on a massive scale. Think about it, Stellan. The ability to control anyone, anywhere. It's not just about money anymore. They have been reshaping the world."

"I just…" Stellan was lost for words.

"They control the world. Alaziah Whalstraus is making it. With some modern-day hocus-pocus and peyote, you got mind control. They front it as an anti-inflammatory drug to help lower high blood pressure. And their ain't a congressperson alive that doesn't have that."

"Military decisions, treaties, ceasefires, annexations of land…" Asher muttered.

"You're getting there," Damian smiled as he saw the two coming to his point of view. "Decisions to go to war. People who decide on a government contract. Making decisions that will later cause terrorist groups to rise and they hire the Clover to go in and clean it up."

Stellan's fists clenched involuntarily. It was like waking up in some twisted nightmare. A man, as far as the world knew, didn't exist and he was controlling everything! "The Iraq War? 9/11? World War I and II?" Stellan thought even further back…" the formation of the United States?"

Damian held out his hand to try and control Stellan. "I know it's a lot to take in. Hell, I know what it feels like. To have your life affected, influenced, or orchestrated to be who you are today? If it hadn't been for The Chairman, would I be who I am today? Would my son be alive? Would millions of people be alive? Would we be living in utopia? Does he purposely cause chaos for money and power or because he serves a higher purpose."

Stellan began to recollect himself.

"It doesn't matter." Damian assured him. "It could be that some of those things happened because of him. Or maybe it happened because it needed to. As a way for nature to fight this imbalance. I'm not a holy man, but I don't believe in coincidences either.

Stellan's jaw clenched; his piercing blue eyes fixed on the bottle of pill. His mind raced, piecing together the implications of what Damian had revealed. The weight of it all threatened to crush him, but years of military discipline kept him focused.

"If CSD can control anyone," Stellan said, his voice low and taut, "then no one's safe. Not world leaders, not military commanders. They could start wars, topple governments... Christ, they could bring the whole world to its knees."

"So, it all leads to this question..." Asher said. Stellan turned to him; he had known Asher for a long time. "What can we do?"

He stood abruptly, pacing the small room. His fingers twitched, itching for action. "We can't let this happen. Whatever it takes, we have to stop them."

Stellan's fists clenched involuntarily. "What do you mean?" Stellan's mind raced, connecting dots he'd never seen before. How many times had his unit been deployed to 'peacekeeping' missions that seemed to spiral out of control? How often had victory felt hollow, as if they were just pawns in a larger game?

"The Syrian civil war," Stellan muttered, the realization hitting him like a punch to the gut. "

Damian leaned forward; his weathered face etched with determination. "Well, it just so happens, the manufacturing of the drug is happening here at a Whalstraus Pharmacy warehouse. I have a guy on the inside. I need you guys to get him out of there. I have everything set up, and I was going to do this myself. But then you two got in the way." He laughed at what he was saying. "I said I was a man who didn't believe in coincidences. And I'm glad you two shitheads got in the way."

Stellan's jaw clenched. "You want us to confront that witch directly?" The thought of facing the witch sent a chill down his spine, but he steeled himself.

"It's risky as hell," Asher interjected, running a hand through his dark hair. "We ship off in two days and we're about to do this?"

Damian nodded grimly. "I've got a way in. Security codes, building schematics. But once you're inside, you're on your own."

Asher looked to Stellan and saw he was all in. "Shit. I guess we are doing this."

Stellan's mind raced, assessing angles, potential threats. "What's our objective? We can't exactly arrest a centuries-old witch, and I'm guessing it's not easy to kill her if she's been around for a century or two."

"My guy is already taken care of most of it. Just get him out." Damian replied.

"And then he'll expose it?" Asher asked. "Putting a target on his back doesn't seem smart to me. Plus, you'll have to be implicated, and you seem like too private of a guy to be willing to be exposed.

As Damian said nothing as he laid out the infiltration plan, Stellan found himself grappling with the magnitude of what they were about to attempt. Everything he thought he knew about the world had been turned upside down. Yet here he was, preparing to dive headfirst into the abyss.

"I really hope you greenhorns are up to be the best American you can be." Damian said his tone grave.

Stellan looked to his friend and then over to his expectant mother of his child, his wife, and devoted friend, Lauren. He looked back on Damian. "Let's fucking party."

CHAPTER 8

Stellan and Asher still couldn't believe they had been talked into this. It had nothing to do with the military, and if their commanding officer heard anything about this, they would surely be court marshalled for this. Stellan could imagine his career coming to an end before it even had a chance to begin, and it all had to do with a shitty camping trip. Why didn't he opt to stay home with Abigail and watch a movie? Stellan even ventured to wonder what his life would have been if he decided to be a football coach instead.

Standing there like a pair of assholes, Stellan and Asher watched as a man in a crisp white shirt approach them as they stood uncertainly in the lobby. He looked nowhere except for them. He extended his hand.

"John. IT Manager. You must be the network engineers from central," he said loudly, for the benefit of the secretary nearby.

Stellan shook his hand, nodding. "Yes, sir. Here to check on those connectivity issues."

John smiled, laughed, and spoke through his teeth, "Shut... up. No one talks like that in IT." He looked around to be sure no one caught them speaking. Then John's lips barely moved as he muttered, "Follow me. Eyes everywhere." He tilted his head subtly toward a camera swiveling their direction.

Stellan's jaw clenched as he fell in step behind John as he led them to the elevator. The oppressive weight of being watched bore down on him. He could feel Asher's tension radiating beside him as they strode down sterile hallways. They were deep in not only enemy territory, but it felt as though SHE was watching them as well. Though the chances of her doing so was slim, he didn't really want to chance anything. It felt as though the elevator took forever to reach the floor. Stellan jumped as the doors behind him opened.

"Stay cool. You guys are from central office. You're supposed to know the layout of the building." John explained he led the way.

Armed guards stood at attention at regular intervals, their hands resting on holstered weapons. Through reinforced windows, Stellan glimpsed sleek drones patrolling the perimeter on the outside of the building. Stellan wondered, careful to keep his face neutral. This place was locked down tighter than any maximum-security prison he saw.

The silence stretched between them as John led them deeper into the facility. Stellan cataloged potential escape routes and defensive positions. But against this level of security, he knew his odds weren't good.

Asher cleared his throat. "Quite an operation you've got here. Must be handling some sensitive data."

John's eyes flicked to a nearby camera before he replied blandly, "Yep, now quit talking." He said through his teeth. They record everything here." Then he said aloud, "Now, let me show you to the server room. That's where I'm having issue with the updates and all. It's asking for some kind of password, and no one on the phone could tell me anything."

"That's why we're here." Stellan clapped John on the back.

John smiled and nodded his head. It was too late to say anything, but he kept his cool as he escorted them to the server room.

The server room door hissed open, revealing a cavernous space filled with blinking lights and humming machinery. John's fingers flew across a nearby keyboard, his movements precise and practiced. Stellan's eyes darted around the room, taking in the rows of servers and the faint smell of ozone.

"Don't worry, I have the cameras on loop in here. All they see in the security room is me sitting at my keyboard." John murmured, gesturing to a monitor. The screen flickered to life, displaying a grainy feed of a subterranean level. "That's where they keep the latest shipment."

Stellan leaned in, his brow furrowing. Crates lined the walls, each bearing an unfamiliar symbol. "What exactly are we looking at?"

John's voice was low and dry. "It's those mind control pills. They call it zeycaine. It's all manufactured here."

Asher shifted uneasily beside Stellan. "Why here in El Paso?"

"They get it from Mexico. Being this close the border, it's easier for the CSD help the cartel smuggle the peyote over."

"I'm sure the president would close the border if he knew about this."

John snorted. "Yeah, that would stop it." He replied sarcastically.

"Well, the border is..." Asher wanted to explain himself.

"I don't care." John cut him off as he continued to prep what he needed to do. "It's here and it's down there. Just get ready for what's about to happen?"

"What are you about to do?" Stellan asked.

"Nothing. Just a magic trick." John replied, pulling out a flash drive. He inserted it into a port, his fingers blurred across the keys once more. A black window popped up on the screen and asked for a password. John typed in ABRACADABRA!!

Stellan watched the progress bar inch forward, his heart pounding. Is this really happening? Was he going to get the evidence he sought out.

Suddenly, John spun around, urgency etched on his face. "Time to leave."

"What's wrong?" Stellan asked, instinctively reaching for a weapon that wasn't there.

"Security and safety protocols are being deleted. The system is deleting everything they have, and I've raised the temperature throughout the building." John explained hurriedly, already heading for the door. "They've probably already sent a guy to ask me what's happening."

Asher's eyes widened. "Are you serious? We've been here for ten minutes and they're already on to us?"

"You know this is an extraction mission, right?"

"I thought we were getting evidence!" Stellan replied.

"No! It's not! Now let's get out of here."

As they rushed from the room, Stellan's mind raced. What did Damian get them into? And how the hell are we getting out?

The moment they stepped into the hallway; all hell broke loose. Red lights flashed, bathing the corridor in an eerie crimson glow. A piercing alarm shattered the silence, its wail reverberating off the sterile walls.

"Shit," Stellan muttered, his muscles tensing. This is bad. Real bad.

John's voice cut through the chaos. "I told you! Now let's go!"

"Wait a minute…" Asher started. Stellan could see the frustration on John's face. "If you were doing all this and knew what was happening, then why the hell did you guys even need us?" He asked as they moved quickly down the hallway, John leading the way with frantic urgency.

The elevator at the end of the corridor pinged. Stellan's heart lurched. As the doors slid open, a familiar face emerged – the guard from the Outpost. Recognition flashed in the man's eyes.

"That's why!" John pointed at the two men.

"You!" the guard bellowed, reaching for his weapon.

John turned and picked up an ash tray stand and hurled it at the guards. Stellan's mind raced. No time to think. Just act. He charged forward, closing the distance in three long strides. John bought them a couple of seconds as the guard's gun was halfway out of its holster when Stellan's shoulder slammed into his chest.

They stumbled backward, Stellan's momentum carrying them both through the floor-to-ceiling window with a deafening crash. Glass shards rained down as they tumbled onto a boatswain's chair suspended outside the building.

The world tilted crazily as Stellan grappled with the guard, the platform swaying beneath them. Wind whipped at his face, the ground a dizzying drop below. As they struggled, the guard's boot hit the winch mechanism on platform, and they quickly began to ascend the side of the building.

Asher's heart pounded as he watched Stellan disappear through the shattered window. He wanted to rush to his friend's aid, but a burly guard blocked his path, eyes narrowed with murderous intent. The guard swung a meaty fist. Asher ducked, feeling the air whoosh above his head. He countered with a quick jab

"John!" Asher called out, desperation creeping into his voice. "A little help here?"

John unfortunately was not a soldier of fortune. All he could think of was to jump on the guy's back and wrapped his arm around the man's throat. The guard kicked off the floor and slammed John into the wall behind him. Nothing broke, but John wished that it had been a lot softer. Asher lunged for the man and drove him back into the wall once more. This time it caused John to lose his grip and he slid down the wall.

The big man stumbled, momentarily stunned. Asher seized the opportunity, driving his knee up into the guard's groin. As the man doubled over, Asher brought his elbow down to the center of the man's back. Causing him to crash to the floor.

"Nice teamwork," Asher panted, flashing a grim smile at John as he helped him off the floor.

"Thanks," John moaned. He did not share in the teamwork enthusiasm.

Their moment of triumph was short-lived. The elevator next to them was making a noise. John turned to it and saw the numbers were changing quickly.

"More company?" Asher asked.

"Nothing to worry about." John assured him as he eyed the fire axe mounted on the wall in its glass box. Without hesitation, he smashed the glass and yanked it free.

"What are you—" Asher began, but John was already in motion.

"Just another magic trick!" John said as he made a powerful swing and broke a sprinkler head above him. Water erupted in a pressurized spray, quickly drenching them both.

"Really?" Asher asked.

"Look!" John pointed at the elevator. "The fire alarms are going off now. All the elevators are heading to the ground floor."

76

"Huh. That is a neat trick."

Alarms blared even louder as the sprinkler system engaged throughout the floor.

***

Stellan's heart hammered in his chest as he clung to the boatswain's chair, its metal frame creaking ominously beneath him. The guard's fist connected with his jaw, sending a jolt of pain through his skull. Stellan tasted blood. Stellan couldn't help but think this guy was taking this a little too personally.

"I told them I should had killed you that day!" He yelled as he threw another fist at Stellan.

Stellan blocked the punch, ducked to the side, and delivered a hard right hook. Looked like those boxing lessons at the base paid off. The guard stumbled, his eyes widening in shock as he teetered on the edge of the platform. He rushed Stellan, the platform moving violently underneath them. Stellan steadied himself and caught the man's arm. With a well-placed shoulder to his chest, Stellan was able to flip the guy over. The platform couldn't take it. The winch broke off. He and Stellan rolled down. Stellan grabbed the side railing and managed to scoop the man by the wrist.

"Climb up! I can't hold you long!" Stellan called out as he tried to save the man.

Blinded by his anger, his loyalty to the CSD, or her personal ego. The man instead pulled the knife from his belt. Stellan saw what he was doing and could not risk it. With no choice he had to let go or they both would have been killed. And he was not about to let his boy grow up without his daddy.

Stellan released his grip and he watched, as the man clawed at empty air. Then, with a gut-wrenching scream, he plummeted towards the ground far below.

The chair groaned. There wasn't much time. Stellan thanked all that time and exercise he got for signing his life away to the military as he pulled himself up. As he did so, he thought the boatswain was going to give.

"Dammit," he muttered as he pulled himself to the roof. Muscles straining, Stellan hauled himself up, rolling onto the relative safety of the rooftop. He allowed himself a moment – just one – to catch his breath before scrambling to his feet. Luckily, the roof's exit was not too far away and that would get him back inside. He panted as he sprinted for the fire escape. He could hear the alarms rising and sprinklers spraying as he continued down the steps. As he did so, he saw a large line of people making their way down the stairs. Except for a couple of torn clothing and some bruises, he still could blend in.

"What happened to you?" A lady asked as she calmly followed the others.

"I fell down the stairs a few minutes ago."

"I believe it. Those sprinklers are flooding every floor, it's making it hard not to slip down the stairs." She explained.

Stellan followed the crowd into the lobby as they were led by CSD guards onto the street. One guard was being held up by two of them. He tried to explain that there were three men they needed to find, but the officer in charge dismissed him. "Get him out of here."

Stellan covered the side of his head, so the injured guard didn't identify him as he walked out of the building.

"Over here!" John called out to Stellan.

Stellan watched carefully as he jogged over to John and Asher who were across the street.

"Stellan!" Asher's relief was palpable. "Thank God."

"We're not done yet." John interrupted, his voice tense.

Stellan's eyes narrowed. "What did you do in there?"

John's face was grim. "This." He held out a detonator and pressed the button. The middle of the building exploded. Shortly afterwards the floor beneath it also exploded.

"What?" Stellan's blood ran cold. "We needed that evidence!" He turned to watch as the building began to collapse inside of itself. The people and CSD guards were running away. Luckily the building was empty. Shortly the ground shook violently. Several people fell and looked around.

"That would be the substructure being destroyed." John explained.

As they ran, chaos erupted around. Stellan and Asher led John away from the building. "Hey!" someone called out to Asher. He immediately stopped and look. It was the guard he and John took on. "That guy!" He struggled. "That's the guy!" he called out to the other guards.

"Shit!" Asher said. as he pushed John forward. The three of them made a beeline to the jeep. John got into the back as the two got in. Stellan's eyes flicked to the rearview mirror. Three black SUVs had peeled out and began to move towards them.

"Shit," Stellan breathed, slamming the accelerator. The jeep lurched forward, tires screeching against asphalt.

They tore through the streets, the pursuing vehicles gaining ground with each turn. Stellan's knuckles were white on the steering wheel, his jaw clenched so tight it ached.

Stellan's mind raced with ideas of what John had destroyed. He needed that data, but right now, survival was the priority.

"Hold on," he growled, wrenching the wheel hard to the right. The jeep fishtailed around a corner, narrowly missing a parked car.

One of the SUVs wasn't so lucky. It clipped the parked vehicle, sending it into a wild spin before it flipped and rolled on to its topside. It slid into the intersection. The other two SUVs swerved to miss it. One car was knocked to the side as the SUV smashed through it as if it was nothing.

Asher leaned forward, scanning the upcoming intersections. His mind was clouded with all the commotion happening behind him as he caught a glimpse of the burning building. Stellan looked ahead as he continued to run through red lights.

"Damnit!" Stellan said as he slammed his fist on the steering wheel. No evidence, a burning building, a dead guy, and nothing to show for it. Now he had to deal with this shit.

CHAPTER 9

"Damn it," Stellan muttered, stomping on the gas. The tires squealed as they lurched forward. In the rearview mirror, he caught glimpses of two sleek SUVs gaining on him.

"These guys don't give up." Asher said grimly, twisting in his seat to keep eyes on their pursuers.

"If you saw our paychecks, you'd see why." John explained.

"You shut up! I'm so got damn pissed at you!"

"Me? What did I do?"

"Really?" Stellan turned around to face John.

"The road!" Asher said as he tugged on Stellan's arm.

Stellan looked back in time to dodge an oncoming car. He jerked the wheel to get them on the main road. His mind raced, trying to process what they needed to do now. Stellan had trouble focusing on the task at hand. He could not believe what he was just a part of. He just knew now he needed a miracle.

"You, okay?" Asher asked, shooting him a concerned look.

Stellan gave a curt nod. "I'm good." He focused on the road as he weaved through the traffic, his reflexes razor-sharp. A taxi swerved into their lane, and he jerked the wheel, narrowly avoiding a collision. The jeep's tires screeched as they fishtailed, but Stellan quickly regained control.

Stellan's eyes darted between the road ahead and the rearview mirror. The Clover SUVs were gaining, their forms cutting through traffic with unnerving precision.

"Are these guys stunt drivers?" Stellan asked, his jaw clenched. He swerved around a slow-moving truck, using the jeep's agility to his advantage.

The lead SUV was closing in, its topside flooding their rearview mirror. Stellan could see the determined face of the driver, a woman with short-cropped hair and a cold expression.

"Hang on!" Stellan shouted, spotting a narrow gap between a bus and a dump truck. He yanked the wheel hard, the jeep barely squeezing through. Behind them, he heard the screech of brakes as the SUV rear ended the dump truck. One left.

But Stellan knew they weren't in the clear yet. The city streets stretched out before them, a maze of potential escape routes and deadly dead ends.

Stellan's eyes darted frantically, scanning the crowded streets for an escape route. He spotted a narrow alleyway to their right.

"Hold tight!" he barked, yanking the wheel hard.

The jeep lurched sideways, tires squealing as they veered off the main road. The alley was a tight fit, brick walls scraping the vehicle's sides as Stellan navigated the serpentine path.

"Jesus, Stellan!" Asher exclaimed, white knuckling the dashboard. "At this rate you're going to do the job for them!"

The jeep bounced violently as they hit a series of potholes. Sparks flew from the side as the jeep bounced from one wall the other. He scrapped a dumpster as they exited the alley.

Asher twisted in his seat, peering through the dust-covered rear window. The SUV was keeping up, but it was badly beaten up as the driver tried to mimic Stellan's maneuvers.

The speedometer climbed past 90, then 100. Stellan's knuckles turned white on the steering wheel as he threaded as he made his way down the alley.

"How you doing back there, John?" Asher asked.

"I'm fine." John replied in a calm manner as he looked forward without an expression.'

"Is everyone like this? Or just the people we know?" Asher asked as Stellan went into another alley with the SUV slowly catching up.

Stellan's gaze snapped forward. Hold on!" he barked, cranking the wheel hard.

The jeep suddenly turned, and Stellan slammed on the brakes. The SUV driver didn't have time to turn as he flew into the alley way towards a dump truck. The driver quickly got out and made his way to safety as the SUV smashed into headfirst. The dump truck reemerged and looked at the driver.

"You still alive?"

"I don't know…" the driver replied with a face full of glass. "Call an ambulance." Everyone else in the back moaned in pain. "Better call a couple of 'em."

Stellan began to drive away. "You think they're okay back there?" he asked, unable to keep the concern from his voice.

Asher turned back, his expression unreadable. "I'm sure they're fine."

Stellan nodded but couldn't shake the unease. That had been a close one.

***

The sun began to settle in the west as the adrenaline began to fade. The jeep rumbled over uneven terrain, each jolt reverberating through Stellan's tense muscles. He eased off the accelerator, allowing the vehicle to slow as they emerged from the pass into a wide, barren expanse. The sky's hues of orange and purple helped ease Stellan's nerves.

Stellan's knuckles were white on the steering wheel as he finally spoke. "I think... I think we're clear."

Asher let out a long, shaky breath. "That was too close, man. Way too close."

"But you guys did good." John chimed in from the back seat. "Not bad for your first time."

Stellan's mind raced, trying to process what had just happened. The warehouse, the chase, the narrow escape - it all felt surreal, like something out of a movie. But the ache in his muscles and the lingering smell of smoke reminded him that this was all too real.

Stellan sighed, feeling the weight of responsibility on his shoulders. "I don't know what to believe anymore, Asher. Everything I thought I knew... it's all falling apart."

The jeep fell silent for a moment, the only sound the crunch of tires on gravel. Stellan's mind wandered to his family, to the oath he'd taken when he joined the military. How had protecting his country led him here, to this moment?

"Whatever happens…" Asher finally said, his voice steady despite his inner turmoil, "I'm sticking by you." Asher placed a reassuring hand on Stellan's shoulder.

Stellan put the jeep into gear. "Thanks, brother." Stellan replied. He knew what he had to do next. At least he felt like it was a solid next move. He needed to see Damian again and get John to safety. There was nothing more for the IT guy to do now. Damian would know what to do with him and he could at least get some answers. He was pissed that they had nothing. All that and no evidence, and he was sure he was going to be arrested. Worst of all, what would happen to Asher? Sure, he said he would be by his side, but he could not help feeling guilty if Asher was arrested too. Asher wanted to leave it all alone and he had to drag his ass along. Why? Just to help him. At least Damian can tell them why he did all this. He owed them that much.

CHAPTER 10

Stellan made it back late that night to the rendezvous point where Damian waited for them. He was standing out in the middle of nowhere under a streetlamp. Stellan felt it odd that he would be out in the middle of nowhere with his guard down, but then again. Damian didn't come off as a guy to be so carefree.

Despite how upset he was with the man. Stellan was relieved to see the old man's weathered face. Years of secrets and loss. Stellan's fists clenched at his sides; his jaw tight as he fought to control the anger bubbling up inside him.

"Why?" Stellan's voice cracked, raw with frustration. "Why the hell did you destroy everything? We could have nailed Clover. Now there's nothing!"

Damian's eyes, pools of weary resignation, met Stellan's gaze. "Evidence?" A humorless chuckle escaped his lips. "Son, have you not been paying attention?"

Stellan's mind raced, struggling to reconcile the enormity of what Damian was implying with everything he thought he knew about the world. Now he could see how an organization could be so powerful. So untouchable. It was because no one would do anything about it. The saying was true. Evil can triumph because good men would do nothing.

Asher could see Stellan was getting angrier by the minute and stepped in. "We had everything. Why?" Stellan backed down. Something about him asking questions allowed Stellan to regain his thoughts.

"The Thule Society," Damian continued, "their influence... it's beyond anything you can imagine. I've seen countries crumble at their whim; entire bloodlines erased from history."

"All the more reason something needs to be done. Stellan could feel his friend's skepticism, knew Asher was fighting against

84

the very notion of such a vast conspiracy. But there was something in Damian's eyes—a haunted look that spoke of unimaginable horrors witnessed.

"You've lost people. Why aren't you thinking of them?" Stellan asked.

Damian nodded slowly; his gaze focused as if he were looking into the past. Angrily he spat. "I am! My family. My closest friends. All gone because I did something once upon a time. I got what I thought was evidence."

The atmosphere seemed to close in around them, the air thick with unspoken tragedy. Stellan's anger ebbed, replaced by a creeping dread. If what Damian said was true, was there any way out of this? How fucked were he and Asher?

"Then I was laughed out of court. I was dumped by the military. Court martialed, then released from prison. I kept at it. My friends abandoned me. My wife left me and took my kids. I pressed on! I kept at them! And each time they hit me harder and harder!" Damian looked down at his fist he shook. He then looked up and smiled wildly with tears in his eyes. "My son believed me though. He tried to help."

Stellan and Asher looked to one another. Behind him they heard John say, "Here we go."

"We did a couple of missions. Here and there. It started out fine. We stopped this, exposed that. We thought we were making some lead-way. Then he got that picture of the Chairman." Damian shook his head as he sought the dark horizon as the sun disappeared behind the mountains. All there was to see was an empty street as the lonely streetlamp burned away with an even lonelier man sitting on the bench. "It's all I have left. A photo of the man that took my baby boy from me." The words hit Stellan at home. Was this his destiny? To pick up where Damian left off and continue until some other dumbass gets caught up in all this and hand him the reigns?

"So, we just give up? Hit them hard and then cut and run?" Stellan demanded, his voice low and dangerous.

"Stellan…" Asher tried to reason with him.

"All I hear is woe is me!" Stellan said in a heated voice. "I'm sorry that you lost your son. Your life!" Stellan continued. "But if anything, that means you got to hit them harder."

Damian's eyes snapped back to Stellan's face, a flicker of something—admiration, perhaps? —crossing his features. "And that's what I did tonight." He said firmly. "I've been fighting a long time here. I don't need a lecture from a kid like you."

"Then what the hell? John said he had everything. Why burn it?"

"Because. The CSD would have found a way to debunk it as a myth and John would either be in prison or dead." Damian said in an absolute voice. "This is a war you haven't been trained for." He spoke. "This is a different one and in time you will learn how to fight it."

Asher's restless energy finally erupted as he spun on his heel, his jaw clenched tight. "This is insane," he spat, running a hand through his short-cropped hair. "The way you talk about this. It just leads you into circles. Pulling more people into this. When does it end?"

"When Thule is gone, and the Chairman is dead." Damian shot back.

He paced the length of the dimly lit sidewalk, each step punctuated by a sharp exhale. Stellan could practically see the gears turning in his friend's head, trying to reconcile what they'd just heard.

"We've been trained for just about any scenario." Asher continued, his voice taking on that familiar tone of determined leadership. "You act like we're up against the devil and his army of hell spawn. Everything has an ending, and this damn well does too!"

Damian let out a bitter chuckle. "You think I haven't tried? You think I didn't exhaust every possible avenue?"

"Maybe you missed something," Stellan shot back. "Maybe you—"

"I lost everything, God damnit!" Damian roared, silencing the room. The outburst seemed to age him a decade in an instant. He slumped back on the bench, the fight draining out of him.

"My wife, Sarah," he began, his voice barely above a whisper. "We were high school sweethearts. Built a life together. Had two beautiful girls and the best son anyone could ask for." He swallowed hard. "It was after my son's murder. I came back to the States. I was approached by the police. They told me they were dead too." Damian sobbed. "I can't tell you how many nights I'm up late wondering why I am still alive." Damian looked away then back directly to Stellan. "All I can think of is that they are just fucking with me." He took a deep breath. "Jesus H. Christ, man! This is worse than death! I want to die. But I will take those bastards with me! You hear me?"

Stellan felt his stomach lurch. The raw pain in Damian's voice was unmistakable.

"My best friend, Tom? He'd been like a brother to me for twenty years." He pointed to Stellan and Asher. "Just like you two are. Turned out he was their plant the whole time. Watching me. Reporting everything." Damian's eyes glistened in the low light. "But I got him. Don't you worry about that. I got him good."

The silence that followed was deafening. Stellan glanced at Asher, saw the conflict written across his friend's face. This wasn't the kind of enemy they were trained to fight. This was something far more insidious.

Stellan's jaw clenched as he processed Damian's haunting revelation. The weight of it settled in his chest, a cold, heavy thing that made breathing difficult.

"Christ," Stellan muttered, running a hand through his short-cropped hair. He saw Damian in a different light now. Asher, searching for certainty to cling to. But there was none to be found.

Damian's gaze locked onto Stellan, recognizing the internal struggle. "It's a lot to take in, I know. But this is the reality you're facing. I wanted to spare you my boo hoo story and shit, but you had to keep on. Just like how you're keeping on the CSD now. Get it?"

Stellan's mind raced, duty warring with disbelief. "He's right." he stated at last, his voice low and controlled despite the turmoil within.

"What?" Asher asked.

"I see what's he's getting at." Stellan paused a moment and considered everything that had been said and heard. "I am the one pushing things." Stellan thought back on everything that happened. "They gave me opportunities to leave it. They backed off and what did I do? I kept pushing them! And now I got you involved. I nearly got my wife and Lauren killed." He remembers the guard that tried to kill him back on the rooftop. "And that guard. He ain't coming back for a sequel either."

"What are you getting at, Stellan?" Asher asked.

"I'm turning into Damian." Stellan said at last. "You don't want me to be like you." He said as he turned to the old man.

"That's right. I don't." Damian replied, leaning forward. "That's why I had John torch and blow everything away. That evidence would have destroyed you and your friend's lives."

Asher scoffed, but Stellan held up a hand. "Let him finish," he said, his tone brooking no argument.

Damian nodded gratefully. "Our only hope is to chip away at their foundation. Small, strategic missions. Gathering intel, disrupting operations, getting to their key assets."

"Like guerrilla warfare," Stellan mused.

"Exactly," Damian said, a hint of approval in his voice. "We strike where they least expect it, then disappear. It's the only way to make a dent in their armor."

Asher shook his head. Was he really hearing this?

Stellan's mind whirled with the implications. Then he thought about something. "It wasn't just about the pills tonight, was it?" Stellan asked Damian.

The tension crackled like live wire as Stellan's question hung in the air. Before Damian could respond, John's voice cut through the silence, sharp and urgent.

"It was to bring Alaziah out in the open." he interjected, his pragmatic tone slicing through the theoretical discussion.

"With the shipment ruined and the recipe for those drugs gone, she's no longer useful to Thule." Damian added. Stellan could hear the enthusiasm in his voice.

"We only stopped one of Alaziah's shipments. She's been doing this for a while. She's got more of the stuff out there." Asher added. Stellan could tell his friend was not convinced about their accomplishment tonight.

"I have a contingency in place. I already have friends all over that."

"Then what do we do?" Stellan asked.

"She's going to make a move. She'll be coming out into the open. Then we will have the opportunity to get her." Damian said.

"Get her how?" Asher asked.

Damian thought about it for a moment. "By any means necessary."

"Sounds good for me. Better than sitting here without thumbs up each other's asses."

***

When they finally pulled up to the safe house, Stellan's heart plummeted. The safe house was barely recognizable, reduced to a smoking ruin. Shattered glass glittered in the moonlight like a field of broken dreams.

"Jesus Christ," Asher breathed beside him as they climbed out of the vehicle.

Stellan approached the wreckage, his boots crunching on debris. The acrid stench of smoke assaulted his nostrils, making his eyes water. Or maybe it was the realization of what this destruction meant.

"Bear!" he called out, his voice hoarse. "Abigail! Lauren!"

Only silence answered him, broken by the occasional crackle of smoldering timber. Stellan's fists clenched at his sides, a maelstrom of fear and fury building within him.

"She made her move" he muttered, more to himself than the others. "Alaziah got here first."

"There's no way to tell…" Asher tried to talk sense to Stellan.

"The skinwalkers didn't do this." Stellan explained. "Look at this. They just tear shit up and the CSD is too busy with a burning building." Stellan was going by his instinct, and he knew he was right. "It was that godless bitch I tell you. Somehow. Some way. She is directly responsible for this."

A muffled groan cut through the eerie silence, snapping Stellan's attention to a pile of rubble near what used to be the living room. His heart leapt into his throat as he sprinted over, Asher hot on his heels.

"Over here!" Stellan shouted, frantically pushing aside chunks of drywall and splintered wood.

There, beneath the wreckage, lay Bare. His imposing frame was a stark contrast to his current state – battered, bruised, and barely conscious. Stellan's stomach churned at the sight of his friend's injuries.

"Christ, Bear," Asher muttered, helping Stellan clear the debris. "What the hell happened?"

Bear's eyes fluttered open, his gaze unfocused. "Warrior?" he rasped, his usually strong voice now barely above a whisper.

Stellan knelt beside him, gently supporting Bear's head. "We're here, man. Just take it easy."

Bear's face contorted with pain as he tried to sit up. "No time," he growled through gritted teeth. "Alaziah... she came like a storm."

Stellan's blood ran cold. "Abigail and Lauren?" he asked, dreading the answer.

Bear's dark eyes, usually so full of wisdom and strength, now held a haunted look. "I tried," he said, his voice breaking. "But she... her magic. It was so powerful. She took them."

The words hit Stellan like a physical blow. He staggered back, his mind reeling.

"How?" Asher demanded, his voice tight with anger. "How did she find this place?"

Bear shook his head weakly. "It is impossible to know. She just appeared. Attacked and left with the women just as mysteriously." He coughed, a ragged sound that made Stellan wince. "I fought, but... she proved to be too strong for me. It was like nothing I had ever encountered."

Stellan's fists clenched, his nails digging into his palms. The pain helped him focus, pushing back the tide of panic threatening to overwhelm him. He locked eyes with Asher.

"She made her move." Stellan stated, his voice low and dangerous.

Asher nodded, his jaw set. "Where do we go?"

"I know we've been through a lot this past two weeks. But I have a feeling that no matter how bizarre all this shit is. The people behind it. Be they a witch, a monster that disguises himself as a human, or if it's just some jackoff. They're all the same and they like the theatrics." Stellan turned to Asher. "She took them to the Outpost. I bet you she's there waiting for you and me right now."

As he helped Asher carefully move Bear to a more comfortable position, Stellan's thoughts were a chaotic mix of fear and anger.

The image of Abigail and Lauren in Alaziah's clutches made his blood boil. He'd been helpless to protect them, but he'd be damned if he'd fail them now. But he knew he had to keep a clear head about this.

Stellan's gaze snapped to Bear, whose labored breathing filled the air. The big man's eyes were glassy, his skin clammy. "He needs help," Stellan growled, "now."

Damian stepped forward; his weathered face etched with concern. "I'll take him to the hospital."

Bear's hand shot out, gripping John's arm with surprising strength. "No," he rasped. "Buzzard! He's the only one that can help now."

"Who's Buzzard? Stellan asked Damian.

"A healer I'm guess."

"Ordinary medicine… cannot help." Bear struggled. "Need... magical healer."

Asher shook his head. "I get all this bullshit has happened, but Bear needs to be in a hospital."

"Trust me, Warrior." Bear insisted, his dark eyes burning with intensity. "This wound... is not natural. Need... shaman. Medicine man."

Stellan's mind raced, weighing options they didn't have against time that was slipping away. He could feel Bear's life fading, could see Abigail and Lauren's faces, twisted in fear. The weight of it all threatened to crush him.

"Dammit," he muttered, then louder: "Okay. Asher, you, and I hit the Outpost. Damian, you, and John get Bear to this Buzzard. If he can't help, find someone who can. Whatever it takes."

Asher nodded sharply. "Look I want to get the girls back." He looked at Bear. He didn't think anything could hurt a man like that. The native lived up to his name and he can see why he was named Bear. "But look at that guy. She tore into him and will do the same thing to us. We can't just head over there with guns blazing. Not without a plan first."

"You're right." Stellan replied. It was times like this he was damn lucky to have Asher. He knew his friend was right. Stellan just wanted to go over there. Punch people and shoot things, and all that would do is get him killed.

"Alright then. What do you have in mind?" Stellan asked Asher.

"Finally! I didn't think you would ever fucking ask me. Give me your cell phone."

As Asher dialed away on the phone, Stellan squatted down and squeezed Bear's shoulder. "Rest. We've got this."

Bear looked at Stellan with the same expressionless face as Stellan had come to know. "I am not going to say I have doubts about this. But I have serious doubts about this."

Stellan grinned as Asher came back to the group. "It's all set up."

"What is?"

"Don't worry about it. I called the guys. They're going to meet us at the Outpost."

Stellan knew Asher could only mean one thing by "the guys". He looked at Asher and wanted to ask him if he thought they were truly up for something like this. But he had come to trust Asher and his wisdom. He called their friends and they said they would be there. If Asher could believe in them, then damn it, he would too. Asher hadn't let him down and stood by his side through all this. Stellan knew in his heart; Asher knew what he was doing.

CHAPTER 11

The Outpost loomed before them, a hulking silhouette against the fading twilight. It was truly a heavy feeling of "You get what you asked for". Stellan was set to in there with guns ablaze, but thoughts of Abigail and Lauren helped keep him calm. Stellan could feel the calm before the storm swelling inside of Asher. It all came to this. A showdown with a witch. As crazy as it sounded, it was the perfect end to two weeks of absolute hocus-pocus bullshit he and Asher had endured.

"You ready for this?" Stellan asked, his voice low and tense.

Asher gave a curt nod. "As I'll ever be to take on the Wicked Witch of the West."

"No shit." Stellan grinned. This was nuttier than squirrel shit.

They exited the vehicle in perfect sync, scanning the area. Stellan could feel his adrenaline on the rise. He stiffened his back and clutched his weapon under his arm. It was time to see what the United States military had to offer them right here. Right now.

The Outpost's existence was surprisingly punctuated by the oppressive silence, broken only by the whisper of wind through dead grass. Though the CSD did quite the job of turning the desolate area into something, only a single structure stood before them. A large barnlike structure. No doubt the women and his unborn child were in there. What worried Stellan was the monster that sat with them and whatever bag of tricks she had ready for them.

"Stay calm." Asher said low and calm. It helped Stellan to have Asher taking point. It was as though he knew Stellan needed him to be for this moment. It was like all the training they did. Stellan was a cool collective guy, but when it came time for work to be done, he wanted to do it hard and fast. Asher was more methodical and relied on procedures and protocols. One of the reasons Stellan relied on him. "Remember your training and we will survive."

Stellan opened his mouth to respond when a figure stepped out of the darkness. His blood ran cold as Alaziah emerged with guards. Creatures that seemed to flicker at the edges, like heat mirages given form. Skinwalkers. The word echoed in Stellan's mind; a concept he'd dismissed as fiction mere days ago.

"Hold it." Asher said to Stellan. He could sense Stellan was wrapping his finger on the trigger without even looking. "I want them back as much as you do. But right now. It's dealer's choice."

Alaziah's lips curled into a predatory smile. "So! You're the little shit stains that been pestering me." Stellan and Asher could hear the disappointment lingering over her words. "Just another couple Damian taking cheap shots and crying."

Stellan's rage began bubbling up inside him. He wanted nothing more than to wipe that smug look off her face, to make her pay for everything she's had her hands in. But he held himself in check. Asher was right, as always, to play it calm and cool. Stellan remembered Asher had a something in store for this bitch.

"Nothing to say?" Alaziah asked. She was trying to provoke them. They both knew it. Neither Stellan nor Asher said a word. She was toying with their emotions, trying to get them betray their plans. Their strategy. She wanted them to act more erratic.

"Oh, the strong silent type." She snapped. "I don't know why you guys are involved in any of this." She shook her head. It was a though she had a headache. "I gave you plenty of opportunities to walk away. Just like that pathetic Damian who thinks he can save the world." She rolled her eyes. "I know he's filled your head with nonsense about what I am doing. But look at it from my point too. You two wouldn't have jobs. You would have never been where you are without, I am doing right now."

Stellan's jaw clenched, his patience wearing thin. "Yeah. Maybe I could have been a contender."

Alaziah's eyes flashed with cruel amusement. She nodded to two of the guards. They pushed the doors open to reveal Lauren and Abigail sitting in the back of a pickup truck. Their hands bound by handcuffs and their mouths gagged.

Alaziah circled the captives, her fingers trailing along Abigail's shoulder. "This is going to be easy. I was hoping to end Damian and his little weasel too. But instead, I had to settle with these two." Then she grinned. Stellan never knew he could hate a grin so much in his life. "I mean three." She looked directly at Stellan. "It was going to be a baby boy."

Stellan moved up, but Asher grabbed his collar. "Quit it! It's bait!"

Alaziah smiled at Asher. He could see she was telling him he was ruining her fun.

Stellan's blood ran cold. He fought to keep his expression neutral, not wanting to give Alaziah the satisfaction of seeing his fear.

"It still can be. I haven't hurt anyone of them yet. But that depends on you."

"You're insane if you think—" Stellan began but was cut off.

"Where is that old fuck? I'm sick and tired of his shit!" She stopped and looked off to the West to the sound of a machine.

The steady thump-thump-thump of helicopter blades sliced through the air, growing louder by the second. A smirk tugged at the corner of Stellan's mouth as he watched confusion flicker across Alaziah's face. They came!

As the helicopter came into view, Alaziah caught a glimpse of Chip in the pilot's seat, his face set in grim determination. Beside him, Clyde was readying a sniper rifle, his eyes scanning the scene below.

"Shoot them down!" Alaziah ordered just as a guard caught one in the chest sending him back ten feet.

A gust of wind blew through Alaziah and her pack. Three more guards went down without a sound. She retreated into the building as the skinwalkers scattered.

The air erupted in chaos as Barks and Liam burst from their concealment, a blur of camouflage paint and foliage. Stellan's heart pounded as he watched his friends charge the unsuspecting guards. He and Asher dropped to the ground and steadied their sights as a gun fight quickly unfolded.

"Stellan, on me!" Asher barked. They moved in perfect sync, training and exercise experience guiding their actions. Stellan's eyes darted between Abigail and the unfolding melee, his mind racing. He could not help but think of the skinwalkers.

Asher seemed to read his thoughts. "I'll cover you," he shouted over the din. "Get to Abigail and Lauren!"

Stellan nodded, grateful for his friend's quick thinking. As Asher laid down suppressing fire, Stellan sprinted towards the captives, ducking, and weaving through the fray.

A guard appeared in Stellan's peripheral vision, raising his weapon. Without breaking stride, Stellan dropped low and stuck the guard in the chest with the butt of his gun. Then without hesitation he brought the tail end up against the man's face as he fell forward. The guard sprawled back on the floor in a clear daze.

Barks, Asher, and Liam were making easy work of the guards. Maybe all that half drunk and half assed training was coming into play finally. God bless America!

He was mere feet away from Abigail when a bone-chilling screech pierced the air. Stellan's gaze snapped to Alaziah. Purple and gray smoke swirled around her as she raised around her. She took in a deep breath and screamed aloud.

It felt like a tornado punched him in the face. Stellan found himself and CSD team too, with his friends being forced out. Her security team had also been blown out too. He guessed she was fed up with them too. Only she and the hostages were inside. Stellan and Asher got up in time to see Alaziah was not done. She focused on the helicopter. With her arm stretched out, wth a rod in her hand and pointed to the ground. A whirl wind formed and hit Chip and Clyde.

The helicopter lurched violently, smoke billowing from its tail. "No!" Stellan yelled, helplessly as he watched Chip struggle to maintain control. The chopper veered sharply, trailing black smoke as it retreated from the Outpost.

"What the hell was that?" Chip asked.

Clyde dropped his rifle and held on to the side of the helicopter. Chip pulled back and lowered the copter close enough to the ground for Clyde to hop off safely. Chip then flew low and fast before anything else could happen. Alaziah fell to one knee as it took a lot of her strength to bring the helicopter down.

With a final, agonized look at Abigail, Stellan retreated to Asher's position. As they huddled behind cover, Stellan's mind raced. "Holy shit!" He looked back at Alaziah. "She could had done that to us the whole time!"

"Yeah." Asher huffed as he looked around the jeep's tire. "Maybe… maybe magic is a real thing."

"Damn it!" Barks said as he came around the corner of the jeep. Liam close behind him. "I didn't think it was a real witch."

"But you believe in this stuff." Stellan reminded him.

"Well yeah. But Chip said we were going after some bitch."

Stellan and Asher rolled their eyes as they let out an exacerbated sigh. "I knew I should have called Clyde instead."

"Barks!" Liam called out. "You're, and I can't believe I'm saying this, the expert about witches. What do we do?"

"Don't forget we got skinwalkers out and about too." Asher added.

"I got nothing." Barks shook his head.

"What? The one damn time I'm willing to listen to your idiotic shit about witches and werewolves, and you got nothing?"

"I'm just a wolf. There's a reason we stay away from their kind."

"That just sounds racist." Asher said. Liam and Stellan nodded and agreed.

"Guys…" Barks was lost for words.

"You need to work on yourself." Liam said.

"The witch?" Barks gestured to Alaziah was getting back up.

"I don't know. I'm kinda disappointed in you right now, Barks. I'm not going to lie." Stellan replied.

"Seriously though. What are we going to do about her?" Asher asked. Barks let out a huff of frustration.

"Oh no. We're going to circle back on your attitude towards other races, Barks." Asher assured him.

Stellan turned his head to see what was happening when a coyote snapped at his face. He fell back. Asher and the other drew their guns and fired, but the bullets only passed through the skinwalkers without phasing them. The creatures closed in, their movements slow and already calculated.

Stellan looked to Asher. He shook his head. He put his gun on the ground.

"What are you doing?"

"Right now, we need a miracle. If we shoot again, they may kill us here." He looked over to Alaziah. She stood looking in their direction. "She wants Damian, right? It's the only thing keeping us alive."

Stellan looked at the skinwalkers as they stood their ground. All of them growling and ready to pounce. Stellan could not help but remember seeing them in their human forms.

They were just kids. Even with supernatural powers they were just kids. He looked into their eyes and saw they didn't really want to kill. The eyes were angry but innocent. They were more than capable of killing, and maybe they have before. Most likely because she forced them to.

This gave Stellan an idea. He put his gun on the ground. Liam and Barks did as well, and they followed Stellan as he reached into the sky and came out behind the jeep. In the distance he could see Clyde being escorted back to Alaziah's position as well.

"Got a bunch of kids working for you, huh?" Stellan asked. Alaziah remained quiet. "I've seen their eyes. Must be hard to make them kill." Still Alaziah said nothing.

"I remember when we all first joined the army. Ready to fight. Ready to kill. Ready to do what we were told." He reminisced. "Then the training started, and we thought we were going to die. Damn they broke us and molded us into soldiers." Stellan laughed. The other only watched Stellan. "But you didn't have to do any of that stuff with them did you?"

"I'm their family."

"No, you're not." Stellan shook his head. "These guys are my brothers. These skinwalkers are just your slaves. As old as you are. You never dropped that 1800s mentality, did ya?" Asher and the others looked at each other to see if any of them knew what Stellan was doing. They simply followed him with the skinwalkers nipping at their heels. "They're just kids. Kids you took advantage of. It's why you want them to stay in their animal forms isn't."

"I will admit that they are easier to handle when they are like this." Alaziah admitted.

"I imagine." Stellan said as he looked back at the skinwalkers with sympathy in his eyes. "I can only imagine what is going through their heads." Then he looked back to Alaziah with disgust and a silent rage. "Just what you put in their heads. Be it words or spells. It just comes up with you being a horrible human being."

"Oh, I am so much more than a mere human." Alaziah replied with a thick layer of narcissism.

A sudden, biting wind whipped through the Outpost. The skinwalkers froze, their glowing eyes fixed on a point. Alaziah's face became drained of all its color. Stellan couldn't help but break his gaze on Alaziah. he turned to see not what she was looking at, but who.

Bear stood before all of them. He was healed, and if he was still hurting his empowering demeanor hid it well. Stellan was both impressed and even feared the power Bear commanded with his pose.

His hair flowed in the wind. His clothes flapped quietly in the wind. His rolled-up shirt was half buttoned up revealing a nasty scar left from a bear, which Stellan surmised lost that battle. He never displayed any emotion. Just told people how he felt. Happy, joking, sad, angry. You never knew with him. It was like reading a rock. But at this moment Stellan knew damn well that he was pissed off. If looked could kill, Alaziah's head would have been blown clear off her shoulders.

"Thank God you came." Stellan let out quietly. The others would have heard him, but everyone was transfixed on Bear.

Standing behind him, Stellan thought it was Damian again. He almost shouted to let him know Damian was not safe here, but a closer look and he saw it was an elderly Native American.

His eyes looked closed, and he leaned on a tall walking stick adorned with feathers and small leather bag. Dressed similarly as Bear, but a belt crossed his moccasin vest at the shoulder. It looked like a gun belt, but he was armed with herbs, small pouches of medicine. Stellan could even see different types of sticks as well, most likely incense sticks varying by smell for different occasions.

The coyotes ran to Bear's location. At first, they all thought they were going to attack the two Natives, but they stopped to a trot. Their heads perked up; they were looking curiously. They felt something familiar about the elder stepped forward as he smoked a long pipe. He and Bear stood silently, looking over the skinwalkers.

The elder Native nodded his head as he looked from one Coyote to the other.

"Kill him!" Alaziah commanded. She had forgotten about Stellan and his company. "I said kill him!" She commanded much more, but it was as though the skinwalkers could not hear her or just ignored her. There was something to this man that threatened Alaziah.

"Why doesn't she kill him?" Asher asked Barks.

"Maybe she can't. I heard of people like him." Barks explained. "He's a natural enemy of any witch. Foreign or not. He must be a healer."

"It has to be Buzzard." Asher interjected.

"The guy Bear wanted?" Stellan asked as he looked on with them at what unfolded. The elderly man looked to Bear.

"I feel them. They are my ancestors." He announced. The Coyotes leaned back and lowered their heads as if ashamed. They looked like they were starting to run when the elder turned back to them with his hands up. "Do not run. Please stay. Listen."

Stellan watched as the oversized coyotes huddled closer together, their expressions a mix of hope and uncertainty. He felt a surge of protectiveness, remembering his own struggles as a young soldier.

"Please. It is time to see you." The elder spoke firmly like a parent who had to decide what to do with a child who had been misbehaving.

Obeying the elder they transformed into their true selves. They were just children, their pack leader looked no more than sixteen. Stellan and the rest looked shocked and gaped at what they saw. They were wearing small moccasin pants. Somewhere shirtless with paint on their skins. Animals Stellan had recognized to be coyotes, eagles, and bears. Animals they could transform into. Some had soft leather shirts. Around their waists were pelts of the animals they had taken long ago. The pelts of predators their tribes had deemed taboo.

Alaziah could still be heard in the distance demanding her skinwalkers to take the life of the elder. She yelled. "Kill him! Just like you killed the others!" At these words the young boys bowed their heads in shame.

"Angry. Scared. I know your story." Said the elder. The boys looked to him with undivided and patience. "My name is Buzzard. I am a healer and medicine man. I am the grandchild of Running Bird and Winema." The boys looked to one another and nodded their heads.

"The Suma, like many others were treated harshly." Buzzard continued. "Many of your friends died of diseases or forced to stay with the Spanish or yielded to the Apache. Attacks from terrible men both white and not." Tears filled in their eyes. All they were not looking for justification for their actions. There were none. They only wanted someone to understand.

Buzzard held out his hands and spoke in a language no one understood. Bear felt it was close to Ulto-Aztecan, but even then, it was hard to understand a language not spoken since the late 1700s early 1800s. Everyone looked on as boys approached Buzzard and fell to their knees, tears swelling in their eyes. The boys nodded and removed their pelts from their waist belt.

This put Alaziah into a rage. She stepped forward, "You ungrateful little shits!" Everyone watched in confusion as Alaziah stomped her way towards the boys. "I took you in! I showed you the way to be powerful and avenge your fallen tribe!" She held up the rod again and pointed at Buzzard and the boys.

"Silence witch!" Bear bellowed as he stepped forward holding a charm in his hand. Everything went silent as the words carried across the air. Alaziah was knocked by an invisible force. She stopped and hissed. "They were boys! Children! Everything taken from them by terrible people. Terrible diseases."

Bear looked to them to see if they were okay. Then back to the witch. Furry burning in his eyes. "It is sad for them and unfortunate that they were born when a new era was upon our people." Bear's monotone carried a weight of sorrow.

"It is unfortunate the men who brought this new era felt there was no place or us." Bear said as he made his approach to Alaziah. She fell to the ground.

Stellan was not sure what Bear was doing, but it was working. He saw Alaziah scratching at the ground in pain. He didn't understand how magic worked, and didn't care to.

"You are no better! You took them young and made promises only a child could believe! You tricked them into committing the taboo of becoming skinwalkers! Forever cursing them to stay with you!" Bear's word tore into the witch. She writhed with pain as she crawled from the healer with each sentence he spoke.

"I know not the origin or what kind of magic you wield, witch! But you will no longer hold power of these youths."

Buzzard spoke up. "Come children. It is time for you to move on. You have suffered long enough in your banishment. I, the last of the Suma forgive you. Please return to your tribe. They are waiting for you. Make haste and find your families."

The boys began to cry. They had waited for hundreds of years to hear words they believed would never come.

A gust of wind blew all around them as their solid beings became transparent in a ghostly blue and white aura. They looked up and in their long-forgotten language, they thanked Buzzard.

The young boys turned to face her, but there were no more tears now. Only anger and resentment. Years of being her servant. Years of exile. Years of taking her orders and doing her bidding. It was time for her evil to end.

Alaziah grimaced as she readied herself for a fight, but then she broke away and began to run. The boys faded as a ghostly wind. Stellan heard the language of the Suma. The voiced of their tribe, angry at Alaziah for taking their children away.

A wind of pure white flowed all around the witch. Puffs of purple, black, and gray smoke appeared, but a swirl of white light engulfed Alaziah and the bodies of the CSD security team. A whirlwind swirled into the air and exploded into shambles of light. She was nowhere to be seen.

Stellan seeing Alaziah was now gone forever, ran to the women with Asher close behind him. Together they were able to untie Abigail and Lauren, and both embraced their husbands. Clyde, Liam, and Barks approached them with Bear and Buzzard behind them.

Clyde opened the tailgate and helped Abigail down, then Lauren. As Stellan hopped out, he asked, "Is that it? Is everything over now?"

Bear nodded. "The skinwalkers and the witch who held them captive are no more. The boys have gone to the spirit world to rejoin their tribe."

"I hope that witch is burning in hell." Asher said.

Bear did not have time to think what happened to anyone good or bad when died. It was a concept he never spoke on because he never wasted time on such a subject when so much living was to be done here and now. He simply looked to Asher and replied with, "Sure."

It was enough for Stellan that Alaziah was no longer among the living. He turned to Bear and hugged him, which Bear remained emotionless and patted him on the back. "Thank you! I could not have done any of this without you!"

"I know." Bear replied.

Stellan looked over to Buzzard. "Thank you too."

"I go where I am needed. Where there is sick or injured. I come to help."

"And you saved the day!" Asher laughed. "I think deep down, Stellan was hoping Bear would come with a friend."

"Damn right. Shit, it was all I had left."

"Stalling always helps." Clyde smiled.

The sound of a helicopter returned to the area. They all looked up to Chip and waved, happy to see he didn't crash.

Stellan's eyes swept across the Outpost. He could not help how eerie the place was now. Not after what he had seen and been through the last several days. He took a deep breath put his hands on his knees.

"Are you okay?" Abigail asked.

Stellan stood up and bent backwards to stretch. It felt the world's weight had been lifted off his shoulders. Everything he had learned and endured made him feel stronger than before. Before this he did not believe in any witches, magic, monsters, or secret societies. It was all nonsense to him, but now. Now he was a believer.

"Stellan?" Abigail asked again. He looked at her as if he hadn't heard her at all. "Are you okay?"

"Damn right I am!" Stellan smiled and held her close to him. He looked down at her with his blue eyes. She was lost in them. She couldn't remember the last time she had seen them so alive with eagerness, ambition, and a sense of adventure. "And everything is going to be alright." He ensured her as he bent down and gave her the most passionate kiss she had ever and will forever remember.

CHAPTER 12

The night before their roll out, everyone had one last party. The raucous laughter of comrades echoed through the lively bar, where Stellan leaned back in his chair, a glass of whiskey cradled loosely in his calloused hand. The air was thick with the scent of stale beer and triumph, mingling effortlessly with the sounds of clinking glasses and boisterous tales of bravado. Each face around him, illuminated by smiles and grins.

Asher, ever the nucleus of their group, stood with a grin plastered across his face, his dark eyes glinting with unrestrained joy as he hoisted his pint high. "Stellan, I have to hand it to ya! When you told me last month that you were going to make everything exciting and fun, I never knew it would have been anything like this!"

"I'm a man of my word!" Stellan replied, the corner of his mouth twitching into a half-smile. His eyes scanned the faces of friends who were more like family, their shared ordeal a silent bond that tethered them all. He stood up.

"He's got something say, everyone!" Chip said aloud so everyone would quiet down and listen.

"When I first joined the army. I was excited. Scared." He chuckled. "I didn't know what I was doing. I thought I was in over my head." He looked to his friends. "You guys. You are not my friends." They all looked to one another in confusion. "You are so much more than that."

They began to relax.

"You guys are family!" Stellan said. Maybe he was a little buzzed. Maybe it was the stress coming off. "No matter how insane I sounded. No matter what I said. Each of you stuck by me. Each of you helped me. Damn well saved my wife and son to be!" He looked over to Abigail. "His name is going to be Blake by the way." He smiled. His friends cheered for him.

"Good name!" Clyde said.

"Thanks." Stellan smiled back. "But you guys are my brothers. I always heard soldiers refer to their friends as brothers. I only thought it was a term of endearment. But I know now why we are brothers." Stellan looked up towards the ceiling. "The army doesn't train us to survive. They don't train us to kill. They don't train us to just follow orders."

"They don't pay a damn either!" Chip added with a sound of laughter following as usual.

Stellan nodded. The army pay did suck, and he let Chip have that one. "But really..." Stellan began again. Everyone quieted down to listen. They could tell what Stellan had to say was important.

"They say an army of one. That is because we ARE one. We are trained to be brothers and to move as a unit. A family. A whole. Whatever you want to call it. I say we are brothers, and we have sisters too." Stellan added looking to Lauren and the other women. He looked to Abigail. "We have wives as well. I used to think we did this because it was merely our duty to protect what is important. I have learned there is weird and dangerous shit out there." He thought for a moment of the Chairman. "We are trained to rely on each other and combat those seeking to destroy everything we hold dear. That is not just our country. It is our fellow brothers and sisters. We fight for America. We fight for the freedom and the love of our family! Sure, we may argue at times, but that's what family does. Because no matter how much we argue, we still love one another, and we protect one another." Stellan held his glass up in the air. "To brothers! To sisters! To family!"

"Here! Here!" His brothers called out and they all took a drink.

It was in this moment of revelry that the television mounted on the wall flickered with the urgency of breaking news, cutting through their celebration like a sharp knife. Asher's hand shot up, motioning for quiet, his gaze locked onto the screen. "Hey, everyone, look!"

The chatter subsided, heads turning in unison towards the anchor's solemn visage as she reported on the blaze that had consumed Whalstraus building—an inferno Stellan and Asher knew all too well. The screen flashed images of smoldering ruins and emergency vehicles.

"Hey Mark! Can you turn up the TV?" Liam asked the bartender. He picked up the remotes and turned the volume up on the TV.

As he did so the reporter's voice became louder as she detailed the zeycaine drug recall. She sighted, "The blood pressure medicine primary ingredient is mescaline. It is said to be comparable with LSD and was outlawed in the United States in the late 70s.

Asher turned to Stellan with a shocked expression. "I guess Damian's friends came through."

Stellan nodded as he listened to the screen showed the anchorman and woman talk about a follow up report. "Similarly, the Regional Manager for Clover Security and Defense, also known as CSD, has also become a person of interest in a joint investigation. Theodore Pikeman is being accused of drug trafficking peyote and San Marcus Cacti into the El Paso area and may be a link to the murder of ATF office, Romero Gomez."

"Neither Alaziah Whalstraus nor Theodore Pikeman could be reached for comment and no representative from the Whalstraus, or Clover Security and Defense has replied to our questions." The anchorwoman concluded their segment.

Then as the news went to commercial break, the bartender lowered the volume. Stellan's jaw clenched subtly, the reality of their actions resonating deep within his core. Seeing it on the news gave him the sense of validation of their struggle. He knew the authorities would never find Alaziah or this Pikeman guy. She was in some other world or dimension. Maybe even Hell itself. Pikeman, on the other hand, was probably having his last conversation with the Chairman, or one of his representatives.

Asher and Stellan shared a smile as their wives continued their conversation. It had been a wild week for them, but Asher's smile told him he would do it again in a heartbeat.

Through the raucous jubilation, a figure of authority edged his way toward the epicenter of celebration. Their commanding officer, a man whose presence commanded respect, approached with an ease that belied his rank. His smile was genuine—a rarity—and his eyes sparkled with a cocktail of pride and relief as he laid a firm hand on Stellan's shoulder.

"Look at you two," he began, voice booming yet warm over the cheers and laughter. "I don't know what on God's Green Earth you two did, but luckily it got chalked up as a training exercise. And I got this!" He held out a medal in a box.

"What that?" Asher asked.

"It's what kept me from giving you two a dishonorable discharge from the military." He started. "I get a call saying that I will be ignoring all that happened, and I would be getting an accommodation for it. If anyone asks me about a stolen chopper or troops doing weird shit one and off the base is considered a military exercise." He stopped and looked at them both.

"I'll have a report on your table first thing in the morning." Asher said. This usually got him out of trouble with the staff sergeant.

"Why write me another report, son?"

"Wha…"

"I already got a report from you earlier today." He looked from Asher and then to Stellan. "I don't know who wrote it, but it detailed everything from the ATF death to whatever the shit you got yourself into. I know neither of you wrote it sense it read like a college kid with a PhD and everything was spelled right." He smirked. "Whoever wrote it was one! Never in the army. And two, never met you guys before." He laughed. "Just tell me you learned something, and it won't happen again."

"We learned something, and it won't happen again." Both Stellan and Asher said in unison.

"Good boys. Now remember you are shipping out tomorrow, so enjoy the time you have now with your friends and loved ones! After all," He took his drink from the bartender. "You belong in Uncle Sam's family now." With that he disappeared into the crowd of people.

Asher looked to Stellan. "You think Damian…"

"Him or someone he knows. He said he wasn't alone in his fight with Thule."

"You know what? I don't want to hear any more about societies or any fucking magic again." Asher shook his head and polished off his mug.

***

The night of jubilance continued. As Stellan surveyed his brothers and family, he caught a fleeting glimpse of Bear's broad back through the crowd. His exit was silent and unobtrusive, a stark contrast to the raucous mirth that surrounded them. A flicker of curiosity sparked in Stellan's heart, propelling him away from the warmth of companionship and into the brisk night air.

"Hey," Stellan called out softly as he stepped outside, his eyes adjusting to the darkness where Bear stood—a solitary figure against the backdrop of the city.

Bear turned, his long hair shifting with the movement, his dark eyes reflecting the faint lights from the bar windows. "Soldier," he greeted, but no accompanying smile, but Stellan could tell by now that Bear was happy to see him.

I cannot thank you enough." Stellan started, the words not quite forming as readily as he'd hoped. He cleared his throat, feeling the weight of gratitude press against his ribs. He found it harder to say what he wanted because he knew deep down this was the last time, he would see Bear.

"Soldier," Bear intoned, his voice calm like the steady flow of a deep river. "You and Warrior are strong. Stronger than you believe in yourself. I know others would falter, but you and your brother have shown courage and great strength. It is an honor to have known you."

Stellan was touched by his words. He hardly ever heard praise that wasn't immediately followed by a joke or a hint of sarcasm. "Where will you head next?" Stellan asked, noting the way Bear's gaze seemed to scan the horizon, as if reading a story yet to be written in the stars.

"I go where I am needed." Bear replied simply, the single word resonating with purpose. "There are others who seek guidance,

109

paths that need crossing. Evil that must be defeated." He turned to Stellan. "Or healed. The wind tells me where such things are."

"Really?"

"No. I have a cellular phone."

Stellan nodded and laughed. There was so much to Bear Stellan wanted to know more about, but he felt it in his soul that this is where their story ends. The chill of the night suddenly less biting as he stood before this man who spoke of life as an endless journey, and he couldn't help but wonder where it was that Bear was going.

"Be safe out there Bear," Stellan said, the respect in his voice as palpable as the handshake they exchanged—firm and meaningful.

"I will, Soldier. May you the spirits watch over you and Warrior." Bear returned, his farewell carrying the weight of wisdom as he always did when he spoke.

Stellan watched Bear's tall figure cut through the dimly lit parking lot, the moonlight casting his shadow long and wavering against the asphalt. Stellan marveled as watch are real man of mystery into a jeep, the heavy door closing with a satisfying thud that seemed to echo into the quiet around them.

"Take care, Bear," Stellan said quietly.

With a nod and a final wave, Bear drove off into the night, leaving Stellan alone with his thoughts and the soft hum of the disappearing jeep.

The laughter and cheers from inside the bar muffled into a distant chorus as Asher stepped out into the brisk night air. He came to Stellan's side as his gaze lingered on the fading taillights of the military jeep that had just rumbled away, carrying Bear toward an unknown horizon.

"You know…" came Asher's voice, tinged with amusement as he pushed through the door behind Stellan. "That was our jeep, right?"

Stellan turned, the corner of his mouth quirking up despite the surprise tightening his chest. "Sonofabitch!"

They both watched the space where Bear had disappeared, their laughter mingling with the soft whoosh of the leaves above. The chuckles tapered off like the embers of a dying fire, and Asher's gaze turned upward to the star-smeared sky. "You know," he started, his voice a blend of wonder and confession, "I had to learn the hard way it looks, but there's more to this world than what we see."

Stellan arched an eyebrow, curious. The night breeze carried the remnants of their laughter away, leaving a silence that felt heavy with meaning. "Me too, brother."

"But there is something I want to know." Asher said as he put his hand over Stellan's shoulder.

"What's that?"

"After everything we saw. Everything we witnessed. Every damn thing we learned…" Asher turned to the bar and put his hands on his hips. "You think Barks is really a werewolf?"

Stellan thought of it for a moment. "Nope."

"You don't?"

"Nah. He's just a fucking idiot."

They burst out laughing.

Asher went back inside. Before Stellan followed, he took another look at the world. He knew tonight was the last night of what he considered normal. Tomorrow he would be on the other side of the planet facing a new world facing new challenges and foes he would never understand. He knew further down the line he would no longer be called Soldier, but Father. It was all changing before him, but then again it was always changing. He had just become aware of it now. It was exciting and frightening all at the same time. He turned at the open door where he saw his friends. He saw Abigail. Even she looked different now because soon she would be called Mother.

Stellan took a deep breath and let it out with a soothing sigh. He knew no matter what the future would hold for him; his brothers and loving wife would be there for him. He stepped inside of the bar and closed the door behind him as he rejoined his family in this night of celebration.

OUTPOST COMPANY

The day has come for Stellan and his group, their shadows stretching like dark omens across the sandy asphalt as they stood rigid among the ranks of soldiers preparing for deployment. The heat was a tangible weight, adding to the burden already resting on Stellan's shoulders— a burden compounded by all of his recent experiences and the anxiety of starting a new life as a family man a year from now.

His thoughts churned with the recent revelations. Yet despite the turmoil inside him, his face remained an unreadable mask, eyes fixed ahead, reflecting his years of disciplined training. Today he was not Stellan, father, or some kid anymore. He was a United States Army marksman. His focus now belongs to his country and his brothers and sisters in arms.

Around them, the military base thrummed with the intensity of organized precision. Massive C-17 Globemaster IIIs and C-5 Galaxy aircrafts loomed like steel behemoths, their cavernous bellies swallowing up jeeps and supplies as ground crews orchestrated the dance of logistics with silent efficiency.

Some of them heading directly to Iraq. Others to aircraft carriers. Depending on their missions and assignments.

"Keep your focus, little brother." Muttered Asher beside him, his voice a low drawl that only Stellan could hear.

Stellan's lips twitched momentarily, the ghost of a smile acknowledging Asher's attempt to take the edge of the situation off. "Go it." He replied, voice barely above a whisper.

As pallets secured with netting ascended into the aircraft's belly, guided by the practiced hands of the ground crew, Stellan couldn't help but admire the choreographed mastery of it all. Every soldier knew their role, every crate and vehicle was accounted for— nothing was left to chance.

"Controlled chaos," Stellan mused inwardly, a paradox that somehow made perfect sense within the confines of the military machine.

The desert air quivered with the thunderous heartbeat of aeronautical beasts. Above, squadrons of F-15 Eagles clawed at the sky, their sleek bodies slicing through the haze, while F-16 Fighting Falcons danced a deadly ballet, engines screaming a high-octane chorus of steel power flexing, predatory eyes scanning the horizon.

Stellan's gaze followed the ascent of these metallic titans, feeling their raw power reverberate in his chest. It was a display of might, harnessed and guided by discipline.

"God bless it all." Asher murmured, squinting against the glare of the sun reflecting off the underbellies of the jets.

"And damn those who stand in his way." Clyde added.

Before another word could be exchanged, a shadow detached itself from the flurry of activity—a non-commissioned officer (NCO) whose stern expression cut through the commotion like a blade. He marched towards Stellan and his brothers, his eyes locked onto theirs with unyielding intent.

"Staff Sergeant Ward, Specialist Corbin," the NCO barked, his voice rough as sandpaper. "You're with me. Let's move."

With a nod, Stellan fell into step behind the man. The hairs on the back of his neck stood at attention, his soldier's sense tingling with the scent of something amiss. They were being led away from the swarm of their fellow troops.

"What did you do now?" Asher asked under his breath.

Stellan only shook his head. He couldn't help think this had something to do with the "fun" he had the last two weeks with the CSD, skinwalkers, and witches. In the back of his mind, something itched at him. Could this be the Chairman making a move on him? Was he on the radar afterall?

They navigated between rows of vehicles and supply crates until the NCO halted before a solitary transport plane. Its gaping cargo hold like the mouth of some great leviathan. The NCO turned, fixing them with a look that brooked no argument.

"Inside," he said curtly, motioning toward the darkened interior.

Stellan's pulse quickened, curiosity warring with a creeping sense of dread. He exchanged a glance with Asher, both men silently steeling themselves for whatever lay within the belly of the beast. The other four just looked from Stellan to Asher, wondering if they too were in some kind of trouble. Chip couldn't help but think this was about him barrowing the helicopter for their "military training". At least that was what was on the report. As they stepped into the cool shadows, the clamor of the outside world faded, swallowed by an uneasy hush that seemed to whisper of secrets yet to be unveiled.

Plunging into the cavernous hold of the C-17, Stellan's boots echoed on the metal floor. He step sounded hallow with a lace of uncertainty clinging. It was empty except for the standard cargo, a jeep. Only them and the NCO were the humans on board. Stellan wanted to grab the guy and make him talk. Was this an ambush? Or worse? An execution.

There, in the deepest shadow, stood a figure incongruous with the military milieu—a civilian dressed not in camo but in the sharp lines of practical field attire. Stellan assumed it to be their Civilian Advisor, someone chosen for her keen intellect and no-nonsense attitude. Someone who knew the layout of the land and people they would meet during their tour. It was a woman of medium height, with raven hair cut short and buisness like that seemed to amplify the sharpness of her hawk-like gaze. Her presence alone was enough to raise eyebrows, but the slight tilt of her head and the half-smirk playing on her lips hinted at a familiarity that went beyond professional boundaries.

"Stellan Ward," she called out, her voice slicing through the hush. "You look like a man who's regretting all those nights he didn't get enough sleep."

"Uhhh." Was all Stellan could get out.

"It can't be!" Chip laughed. "Damn, must be luck of the Irish on you, boy!"

"Married life treating you well or is it the thought of diapers that has you looking so grim?" She laughed.

"This is Ezra Cade. She will be your advisor." The NCO explained and then departed for his task.

It felt as though he was struck by lighting. Or at least the butt of someone's prank. Stellan allowed a terse smile to form, his eyes narrowing as he measured the undercurrents of her jest.

"Ezra?" he whispered. It felt like a punch in the stomach. He hated that he sounded like a little school boy trying to talk to his crush. This was not fitting of a soldier.

"Sharp as ever," she quipped. They guys all laughed and elbowed each other, but stopped immediatly when Asher looked crossly at them. This was not good.

"Don't worry so much. Relax. I hope being a married man hasn't made you soft." Ezra joshed.

"If anything. I'm better man for it." Stellan replied, his attention still fixed on Ezera. He was beginning to feel more confident. He was not about to let her question anything. Especially when it came to Abigail.

Ezra smiled as she sat down and withdrew a laptop from her bag. She flicked it open. The soft click of keys cutting through Stellan's thoughts. It felt the world was becoming numb to him as he tried to figure out how a ghost from his past was standing right here before him.

"Communications are secure. Everything is ready, sir." Ezera muttered to the screen. Whatever was happening now, Stellan felt the weight of uncertainty press down—thick, suffocating, inescapable.

The screen flickered once before stabilizing, revealing a figure cloaked in shadows, barely more than a silhouette against a nondescript background. Stellan swallowed and if it werent for the American Flag behind him, he would had thought the Chairman was there to greet him. The fact this was an American talking to him allowed him to unpucker his asshole a bit.

"Hello, men!" The voice was distorted, electronically masked to erase any hint of identity, yet it carried a tone that demanded respect. "You boys have had quite a week."

Stellan's jaw set, muscles tensing as he absorbed the phantom commendation. He and Asher exchanged a quick glance, both their minds churning with the same silent query: Who the hell is this?

Asher shrugged. Stellan didn't even check with the others. If Asher didn't know, they sure as hell were out of the loop.

"Thule Society," the shadowy figure continued, the words dropping like stones into still water, rippling with implications. Stellan could feel his skin tingle as sweat began to bead up on his brow. He looked at Asher, the color had been drained from his face. "I thought that would get your attention." Though Stellan couldn't see it, he knew there was a smile on his face. "Glad to see someone put a boot up their asses."

"Sir?" Stellan asked. But Ezra put her finger to the lip and made a silent shushing gesture. Stellan thought wise to follow her advise. Stellan could feel this guy probably didn't like interruptions.

"Ancient rituals, modern influences, and a strong global network." The shilloutted man continued as if he didn't hear Stellan.

"Dangerous sonsofbitches. And they got magic on their sides! Who would have guessed?"

Asher shifted beside Stellan, a frown creasing his brow. Stellan already could tell Asher had an idea where this was going, and wished he could let him in on the secret. Instead he just followed his big brother's steps and remained quiet.

"Being well trained and wondering what all this is about, you all probably read Damian's report." He said knowing they had without them answering. "Well you lot seem to be diamonds in the rough to that guy. He's a good operative of mine, but unfortunately too old to keep at it." He continued.

"But he as the game goes, he found me a good replacement. And it came with accessories as well!" Again Stellan could feel that invisible grin.

Shit. Was all Stellan could think of. He didn't have to look to Asher to see if he won the prize for guessing what was about to happen.

"I'm forming a team and there is no backing out. Even if you wanted to. You are all now participants of a war like no other. Weird things are out there. And we protect America from them." He paused and what came off as a cheerful demeanor now turned to a very serious tone. Stellan. Asher.

"You know there's a very dangerous man out there. We are what is left of the resistance. A small, but effective group. But we need operatives out there."

"What a minute." Stellan cut in shaking his head.

"Operatives?" Cylde looked to the others then to Stellan and Asher. "What the hell did you get us roped in to?"

"I don't know about this." Chip sounding serious for a change.

The sound of the plane's cargo hull closing tore Stellan and his brothers away from the screen. The man could sense their panic and raised his hands in a stopping gesture to quill them.

"Not to worry. I represent an organization embedded in our government. You will all lead normal lives within the military."

"Wait…" Stellan tried to cut in.

"Routines will be the same and it will feel like you are at home." He continued on, ignoring Stellan. "You will be called upon when your missions overlaps ours, and they will. From this point on, you will be a government taskforce called Outpost Company. We will be in contact."

As the transmission cut, the room plunged back into silence, save for the distant roar of jet engines outside began to turn up. Stellan's heart hammered against his ribs, a primal drumbeat that paced his racing thoughts.

Stellan looked to Ezra, "And how do you fit into this?"

"Why I will be your handler." She replied with a smirk on her face. "Never thought you would be taking orders from me, did you?" She snapped the laptop shut with a definitive click, severing the last tendrils of the man's farewell. She picked up her bag and tucked the laptop away inside.

"Don't worry, boys." she said, her voice threading through the cabin with an edge of steel softened by an almost maternal concern,

"I'll always be a call away."

"Sure," Asher replied, the words edged with sarcasm that didn't quite mask his unease.
"Because this is all normal, right?"

Ezera's lips twitched in what might have been the start of a smile, but it didn't reach her eyes. Those dark orbs shot into Asher's conciousness. "it is. You just only saw what you wanted to see. That's all," she quipped, standing up. Her silhouette cut a sharp figure against the metallic backdrop of the plane's interior as she moved toward the exit. "I'll be seeing you soon."

Stellan watched her go, the weight of her departure settling heavily on his shoulders. As the door closed behind her, the reality of their situation felt impossibly dense. It was as if the air within the aircraft had thickened, charged with the residue of things unsaid and deeds to come.

Their moment of reflection was cut short by the arrival of another NCO, his boots thudding solidly against the metal floor. The man's face was set in a stoic mask, betraying no hint of what churned beneath the surface. He brought with him a presence that commanded attention, an aura that spoke of many years and many secrets.

Who the hell is this guy? Stellan thought, but seaid nothing.

"Corporal Stellan Ward, Saregent Asher Cortez?" He addressed them formally, his voice a low rumble.

"Present," Stellan acknowledged, straightening up.

"This is Yasir Osman. He is going to be your civilian advisor." The NCO explained.

As the plane began to ascend into the air, Osman began to explain what they were going to experience. He spoke of the cities, traditions, and the history of Iraq. Anything that would help them.

As he spoke Stellan looked up at the roof of the cargo wondering why this was happening to him. He couldn't help but wonder if this was his life now and worried if he was going to end of up like Damian. New fears began to arise within him. He wanted answers again, but worried what he would find. More questions most likely. The worst feeling was, everyone he cared about: his family and his brothers were now going to be a part of all this. He took in a deep breath and exailed.

He looked to his brothers as they pretended to be interested in Osman's words, but it was just to be courteious. They knew he was taking a big risk and would be seen as a traitor to many in his country. Stellan watched as he spoke with confidence.

He could tell Osman felt he was doing the right thing, and in a way it was inspiring to him. It made it feel what he was doing now was the right thing. For country, his brothers, and his family to be. If this man, with no military training or experience. Let a lone what war truly was.

By all means in Osman's point of view, Stellan and his brothers should be considered his enemies since they are going to his country to raise hell against Saddam. But instead he went against the grain and wanted to help them. If he could suck it up and do that. Then Stellan felt he could stop his whinning and take the fight to Thule and their feared leader, The Chairman.

MK ULTRA

Oringinating back to the 1940s, Nazi scientist began human experimentation in the concentration camps. Their goal was to develop a "Truth Serium", using phycidelic drugs such as mescaline. A chemical compound found in cacti such as peyote and San Pedro. Their goal was to eliminate the will of their subjects.

After World War II, new threats to the United States had risen. Countries such as Soviet Union, North Korea, and China began research and development into the subject of mind control.

The Central Intelligence Agency believed if mind control was to become a new weapon in the Cold War, then the United States would need to understand and counter this unique tactic. If not be the country who would excel in such practices.

Acting director of the time, Allen Dulles, placed Dr. Sydney Gottleib, CIA chemist, to head up the project. He would go on to expand the Nazi experiment with the use of mescaline. He had Uncle Sam foot a bill of $240,000 ($4.2 million today) for the German created drug Lysergsäure-diethylamid, better known as LSD, to the United States.

This unfortunately was how the United States became exposed to the drug, which is popularly used in night clubs across the country to this day. It was later banned in the late sixties, only to be allowed for use of rituals by the Native Americans, but would later be completely banned in the 70s when Project MK Ultra was finally ended.

To this day, the experiments of MK Ultra and its predecessor, MK Search, has been a failure. The results is damaged minds of countless unwitting participates and prisoners whose minds have been permentaly damaged from the excessive use of LSD.

With further sorrow, the failed Project of MK Ultra continues to be a skeleton in the CIA's closet. Though the agency would go one to have success in their field, one can never truly speak of the CIA without mentioning or thinking about their faluire to create a mind control drug.